Looking for X

QUEEN ANNE HIGH SCHOOL LIBRARY

Also by Deborah Ellis

The Breadwinner
Parvana's Journey
Mud City
The Heaven Shop

DEBORAH ELLIS

{*}{*}{*}

Looking for X

OXFORD
UNIVERSITY PRESS

To Rachel and Rebecca,
with love and gratitude

OXFORD
UNIVERSITY PRESS

Great Clarendon Street, Oxford OX2 6DP

Oxford University Press is a department of the University of Oxford.
It furthers the University's objective of excellence in research, scholarship,
and education by publishing worldwide in

Oxford New York
Auckland Cape Town Dar es Salaam Hong Kong Karachi
Kuala Lumpur Madrid Melbourne Mexico City Nairobi
New Delhi Shanghai Taipei Toronto

With offices in
Argentina Austria Brazil Chile Czech Republic France Greece
Guatemala Hungary Italy Japan Poland Portugal Singapore
South Korea Switzerland Thailand Turkey Ukraine Vietnam

Oxford is a registered trade mark of Oxford University Press
in the UK and in certain other countries

Copyright © Deborah Ellis 1999

The moral rights of the author have been asserted

Database right Oxford University Press (maker)

First published in Canada by Groundwood Books
First published in the UK by Oxford University Press 2006

All rights reserved. No part of this publication may be reproduced,
stored in a retrieval system, or transmitted, in any form or by any means,
without the prior permission in writing of Oxford University Press,
or as expressly permitted by law, or under terms agreed with the appropriate
reprographics rights organization. Enquiries concerning reproduction
outside the scope of the above should be sent to the Rights Department,
Oxford University Press, at the address above

You must not circulate this book in any other binding or cover
and you must impose this same condition on any acquirer

British Library Cataloguing in Publication Data
Data available

ISBN 13: 978-0-19-275417-2
ISBN 10: 0-19-275417-3

1 3 5 7 9 10 8 6 4 2

Typeset in Adobe Garamond by Palimpsest Book Production Limited,
Polmont, Stirlingshire
Printed in Great Britain by Cox & Wyman, Reading, Berkshire

ONE

WHO WE ARE

Mom used to be a stripper.

She quit when I came along. She calls it exotic dancing, which isn't quite right. It is dancing, but exotic doesn't mean dancing while you take your clothes off. Inuit dancing could be exotic, but that's not what Mom did.

She made good money at it, but it all sort of drained away. Before I was born, she was poor, and we've been poor ever since.

A lot of people think that just because Mom used to be a stripper, her children are screwed up and will stay screwed up for ever. Not so. My brothers would have been the way they are no matter how Mom paid her rent.

If I'm screwed up when I become an adult, it will be my own fault. If I'm screwed up now— well, I'm not, so there's nothing more to say about that.

Sometimes strippers get to travel. I'd like that.

Mom says, though, that in all her years of travelling as a dancer, all she saw of the world were two-bit Ontario towns and their two-bit taverns, and there's more to the world than that.

As if I need to be reminded.

I asked Mom once if she thought being an exotic dancer would be a good career for me. She said definitely not.

'It involves dressing up in frilly things, which you hate, and working in nightclubs full of cigarette smoke, which would be bad for your lungs.'

She also said I'd have to deal with a lot of jerks. I wouldn't mind that so much. I deal with a lot of jerks now. I'm pretty good at it, for an eleven year old.

Anyway, I nixed the idea of becoming an exotic dancer. For a while I wanted to be a truck driver, then an aeroplane pilot, then a sailor. The problem, though, with all those careers, is that you have somebody telling you what to do, and you actually have to do work.

I don't like to work, and I certainly don't like anybody telling me what to do.

What I really like to do is wander around and look at things, and then think about them.

It was Mom who first said I should be an explorer, and as soon as she said that, I knew it was true.

I'm going to explore everything, all over the world, from the biggest country to the tiniest island. I already have my own atlases. I'll see things no one else has ever seen, or ever will see. I'll have a new adventure every half hour, and everybody else's life will be really boring compared to mine.

When I take a break in my explorations, I might, if I was begged, agree to give a lecture on what I've seen, but only if someone gives me a lot of money, treats me like a big shot, and buys me a nice dinner.

Mom's name is Tammy, which means perfection. She reminds me of that whenever I disagree with her.

She lets me call her Tammy, or Mom, or Mommy (although I only call her that when I'm not feeling well). She hates being called Tam. She says my father used to call her that when he wanted something, like, 'Hey, Tam. Make me a sandwich.' She doesn't like thinking about my father, even though she's probably reminded of him every time she looks at me. I look like him.

'You remind me of you,' Tammy said once, when I asked her about it. 'Worry about something worth worrying about.'

My brothers look like Tammy. I'm glad they don't look like their father. I didn't like him, and he didn't like me, and I was glad to see him leave when Tammy told him she was pregnant.

My name is Khyber. It's not the name I was given when I was born. That name is so unspeakably horrible that I shall never speak it, not even under torture.

Khyber is the name I have given myself, and Khyber is what everybody calls me. Tammy even registered me at school that way.

Tammy prefers my unspeakable name (naturally, since she chose it), but she understands about me using another name. When she was a dancer, she used a lot of other names. Sandy Sherlock is my favourite. She wore a Sherlock Holmes hat and held a big magnifying glass in her hand. It wasn't a real magnifying glass, though. Those things cost a lot of money, at least the big ones do. I never saw her dance that way, of course, but I've heard the stories.

Mom calls me Khyber. She used to call me the unspeakable name when she was angry with me, but I told her that wasn't fair, so she doesn't do it any more.

I call myself Khyber after the Khyber Pass in Afghanistan.

The Khyber Pass is a wild, dangerous place, full of bandits and history. It's a narrow valley that runs between high mountains, and I'm going to go there some day. I'll stand in the middle of the valley, and everyone passing through will come up to me and ask, 'What is your name?' and I'll say, 'My name is Khyber, and this is my Pass.' Maybe they'll believe me and maybe they won't, but they'll go away thinking they've met someone who's very important indeed.

My brothers' names are David and Daniel. We call them David and Daniel. Sometimes people call them Davy and Danny, but I don't like it, and I don't think they do, either.

They're twins. Most people can't tell them apart, but most people aren't as smart as Tammy and me.

I don't know if they have other names for themselves or not. They hardly ever talk. They're five years old, so everyone thinks they should be talking, but I figure they have nothing much to say just now. Besides, I talk so much that when they're around me, they never have a chance to get a word in.

The twins have autism.

Nobody knows what causes autism, but what it means is that my brothers are more often inside their heads than out of them. That makes it hard for them to learn anything, because to learn something, you have to stop thinking your own thoughts long enough for the new information to reach your brain.

Mom reads a lot of books on autism, looking for ways to get the boys out of their heads. When she isn't reading about autism, she reads about everything else. She says she's trying to decide what she wants to be when she grows up. She thinks she's funny.

Sometimes I let her think so.

The only thing I don't like about the twins being autistic is that they're still in nappies. I don't like changing nappies. Tammy does it most of the time, but sometimes she gets too busy, and then I have to do it. I hate that.

We live in the Regent Park section of Toronto. Regent Park is one of those Cape of Good Hope names. The Cape of Good Hope is the name of that bit of water off the southern tip of Africa.

It used to be called the Cape of Storms, because it's always stormy there. The name was changed to Cape of Good Hope so it wouldn't frighten the sailors. I'll bet, though, that not a single sailor going round the Cape of Good Hope was fooled by the change of name.

A regent is someone who rules a country until the real queen or king grows up. A regent is very rich. Everyone in Regent Park is poor.

'They should have called it Pauper Park,' I said once to Tammy.

'No one would want to live here then,' she replied.

'Hardly anyone wants to live here now,' I answered.

TWO

THE STRANGER AT
THE TABLE

I love coming home from school. A lot of kids don't, but I do. Tammy is always glad to see me. She doesn't make a big fuss about it, but I know she's glad. I think she'd be glad to see me even if I didn't take one of the twins off her hands.

I always know what to expect when I get home.

We live on the top floor of a three-storey red-brick apartment building, right on the corner of Parliament and Gerrard. It's a perfect corner. The library is right across the street, and there's a little park across from that. The grocery store is a short way up Parliament Street (although it seems like a long way when I'm carrying bags of groceries home), and the Goodwill used clothing store is on the other corner.

The apartment faces west, so by the time

school's out, it's filled with warm light. Mom's usually there with the twins, unless they have a doctor's appointment. When I walk through the door, she'll be hanging out with them in the living room, and one of her Monkees records will be playing on the record player.

Tammy's a big Monkees fan. I think she named David after Davy Jones, one of the Monkees, but she denies it. I'm the only kid my age in the whole universe who knows the words to every single Monkees song. Unfortunately, this kind of thing never comes up in exams.

After I grab a snack and complain to Tammy about school, I take one of the twins out with me—David one day, Daniel the next. Mom says it helps her because she uses the time to work with whichever brother stays home, and it helps the twin I take out because he gets extra exercise, which helps him sleep at night, which helps all of us sleep at night. It helps me, too, because after sitting all day in school, I just have to get out.

For a while, Tammy made me go to after-school clubs, but now that I'm eleven, I don't have to any more. They're good for some things, but I have to get along with people all day in school. The strain of it gets to be too much.

Some people are all right, but on the whole I prefer my own company.

That's handy, for an explorer. We explorers are solitary figures. We prefer to be where the crowd isn't.

It was a warm autumn day, that time in October after Thanksgiving but before Hallowe'en. I shuffled along in the dead leaves in the gutter on my way home.

My friend X was sitting in the little park across from my building.

I don't have a whole lot of friends, but the ones I have really are friends. Some girls reel off a long list of kids they call their friends, but most of them are just names to invite to a birthday party. They're nobody special.

My friends are special. X is certainly special.

I never know when she'll turn up. I don't know where she goes when she's not with me. I don't even know her real name. I call her X because X sounds mysterious, and my friend is mysterious. She won't tell me her real name, or anything about her life. She's afraid of the secret police.

'Which secret police?' I asked her once.

'All of them,' she replied, which is an awful lot to be frightened of.

I walked right past the park, pretending not to see her, and she pretended not to see me, just in case the secret police were watching.

I have my own set of keys, one for the apartment and one for the outside door. I keep them around my neck on a cow-coloured shoelace Tammy found at the dollar store. I usually wear it under my shirt, so that some creep won't get the idea that I'm alone in the apartment sometimes. It's a safety thing.

The teenagers hanging around the entrance ignored me as I unlocked the building door. They're too cool to bother with a kid like me. They're too cool to bother with anything. They're probably too cool even to breathe. They always hang around the entrance, draped over each other. Now and then I check them out to see if moss is growing on them.

'Nice day,' I said.

'Huh?' one of them grunted, almost collapsing from the effort.

I laughed and went inside. I'll be a teenager soon, but I won't be like them. I couldn't bear to stand still for that long.

Glad the school day was over, I opened our apartment door.

A strange woman was sitting at our kitchen table. The Monkees were not singing.

The twins were in the kitchen, too. David was on his knees by the cupboards, in his favourite rocking position. There was a pillow on the floor in front of him so he wouldn't hurt his head if he rocked too hard. Daniel was hopping in one place, flapping his arms like he was a baby bird trying to fly. I gave them each a hug, although I knew they wouldn't hug me back.

There was a heavy feeling in the apartment, and I felt I had just walked in on something very bad.

'I'm home,' I said to Mom, which was a dumb thing to say, since I was standing right in front of her.

Mom barely glanced at me. Her face had that tight, pinched look it gets when she's trying not to cry. I've seen it on her face when we're out in public, the twins are acting up, and she's tired, or when she gets angry at someone who says something stupid. She says when she gets angry she feels like crying, but doesn't want to cry. She didn't look angry today, though, just sad.

The strange woman smiled at me and said,

'You must be (unmentionable name).' I saw the briefcase at her feet. The only people who come to Regent Park with briefcases are social workers. I started to ignore her.

Tammy cleared her throat. It was her we-are-polite-to-guests-in-this-house noise. I mumbled hello. That was as polite as I was going to get.

The twins' button collection was all over the floor. They can play with their buttons for hours. They look at them, spin them, and let them drop like water through their fingers. Mom says it's part of their autism, to play like that for hours on end. She keeps trying to get them to do other things, like use crayons, but I don't think it's such a bad thing for them to play with buttons. They could spend their time doing worse things, like trigonometry, or building bombs that would destroy places I haven't explored yet.

'No buttons in your mouth,' I said to Daniel, fishing it out. I rinsed it in the sink and dropped it back on the pile.

'My friend is waiting for me,' I said to Tammy as I made X a peanut butter and corn syrup sandwich. X likes my sandwiches. I've never seen her eat anything else. She worries that her food could be poisoned by the secret police.

The social worker had spread her papers all over our kitchen table. I considered pouring corn syrup on them, but then there would be none left for sandwiches.

I wrapped the sandwich in a piece of newspaper and put it in my shoulder bag, then fetched David's jacket and started to put it on him.

'David's going to stay here this afternoon,' Mom said.

'It's his turn, I took Daniel out yesterday.'

'Daniel's staying here, too.'

'But I always take one of the twins out after school.'

'Well, today you don't,' Tammy snapped, then immediately looked embarrassed. It took me a moment to realize she was embarrassed because the social worker was there.

It made me mad that this strange woman with the briefcase could make Mom feel bad.

It made me livid to then see the social worker put an ugly, claw-like hand on Mom's arm, as if to comfort her, and Mom let her do it! If any social worker did that to me, I'd slug her. I'd be in horrible trouble, but it would be worth it.

'You have the afternoon to yourself,' Mom said, in a voice that was a little too loud and a little too cheerful. I could tell they wanted me to leave.

Naturally, that made me want to stay.

If X hadn't been waiting for me, I would have pulled up a chair, just to make them angry. But I couldn't let X down.

Without saying goodbye, I left.

'I'll show her,' I muttered, closing the apartment door as noisily as I could without actually slamming it. Slamming the door would get me in trouble. 'See if I ever take the twins out again.'

But that was just grumbling. Of course I'd take the twins out again. I liked taking them out.

THREE

A TREE FROM BRAZIL AND
A WOMAN FROM NOWHERE

X was gone, but I knew she would be. I also knew where to find her. She'd be sitting on a bench in Allan Gardens, the big park down the street.

Allan Gardens is not full of people named Allan. It's full of trees and squirrels and people who sleep on park benches. They may all be named Allan, but I doubt it. Anyway, anybody can use the park, no matter what their name is.

I didn't see X on any of our usual benches, so I headed into the giant greenhouse in the centre of the park. She was sitting on a bench in the huge entrance room, hunched into her grey trench coat, as usual, looking down at her feet instead of at the plants around her. Her blue suitcase was on the ground, tight between her feet.

X is pretty old. She has short white hair, and her face is full of wrinkles.

I sat down on the other end of the bench and put the sandwich between us. Slowly she reached out and pulled the sandwich towards her. While she ate, I talked.

X is like the twins. She listens to everything I say, but hardly ever says anything herself. Sometimes she answers a direct question, but it makes her look so uncomfortable that I don't ask them very often.

'There's a social worker sitting at our kitchen table,' I said. 'She's got three heads, and claws, and she smells bad.'

X nodded as she pulled her sandwich apart and looked at it closely. She trusted me, but she liked to be careful.

'I hate social workers,' I continued. 'They talk to Tammy as if she were a bad mother.'

'It's not just me,' Tammy once told me. 'They talk to all people on welfare that way. It's because we take money from the government.'

That may be true, but some things are just for Tammy. I've heard social workers say, 'I see from your file that you used to be a stripper. Hmmm.' Then they sneer at Tammy as if they were waiting for her to apologize. She never does, though.

X stopped eating, and I realized I had stopped talking. She feels more comfortable if I talk while she eats. I think it helps her feel invisible, because while I'm talking, I'm paying attention to other things, not to her. If you're being chased by the secret police, invisibility is useful.

I started talking again. Since we were sitting under a tree from Brazil, I told her about some of the strange animals found in the Amazon jungle. I exaggerated a bit—there isn't really a five-hundred-pound frog—but X didn't seem to mind.

X and I left the greenhouse separately, as always. I headed towards the library. I don't know where X went.

It felt funny being out on my own on a weekday. I always had one of the boys with me, their harness strapped to my wrist, their hand in mine. It felt weird to be alone, but it felt good, too. I felt free.

On the way to the library, I stopped by an Italian restaurant. It had a menu posted outside. I stood and read the menu. I was hungry. I'm always hungry. Tammy feeds me, of course, and I get food at the lunch-and-breakfast club at school, but I'm always hungry anyway. Sometimes my hunger is so big I feel that I can eat everything I see—dogs, cars, park benches, newspaper boxes—just swallow them whole.

I read over the menu and decided on a ravioli dinner, with a side order of chicken and a double dessert. It would cost as much for one meal as it cost us to buy groceries for a whole week.

Someday I'm going to have enough money to be able to walk into any restaurant in town and order whatever I want, and keep ordering and eating until I can't eat anything more.

In the library I spent an hour looking at the big atlas. I never go into the library when one of my brothers is with me. They make too much noise, and they bother other people. The librarian asked me not to bring them. I wanted Tammy to complain, but she said she has too many other things to worry about.

Through the library window I saw the social worker leave my building. Social workers always look like they're dying to wash their hands when they leave our neighbourhood.

I went home.

Mom was sitting in the living room with the twins. Our living room has no regular furniture, just mattresses along the walls, covered with blankets and lots of colourful pillows. Making pillows is a hobby of Tammy's. She gets clothes from the second-hand store on dollar-a-pound days, and cuts them up into shapes and sews them back together to make pillows. They're really pretty.

We don't have a television. We used to, but Mom had to sell it to get money for a treatment for the boys. I don't really mind. It didn't work very well, anyway.

The twins were curled up with Tammy, making their little noises and playing with their fingers.

'If they're quiet now, they won't sleep tonight,' I said.

Mom smiled me a hello smile. 'We'll worry about that tonight. Right now, I want all my babies close to me.'

I like it when she calls us her babies. It's kind of a dopey thing to say, since we're not babies, but I like it anyway.

I joined them on the mattress and we all snuggled in. We might have stayed like that all night, but my stomach let out a huge rumble, so Tammy decided it was time to light the fire under the soup. She meant turn the stove burner on. There's no actual fire. We have an electric stove.

We almost always have soup. Even if we don't have it for dinner, it's always around. Tammy makes it herself and puts everything in it, but lets me pick out any lima beans I find. Sometimes we have soup and bread, sometimes soup and sandwiches, sometimes soup poured over mashed potatoes. On this night, we were having soup poured over little squares of toasted stale bread.

While Tammy made the toast and cut it into squares, I stirred the soup and sang the soup song:

'Beautiful soup, so rich and green,
Waiting in a hot tureen!
Who for such dainties would not stoop?
Soup of the evening, beautiful soup!
Soup of the evening, beautiful soup!'

It's the Mock Turtle's song from *Alice in Wonderland*. We made up the tune. Sometimes we make up other words to it.

'Horrible soup, so slimy and foul
Made with the head of a wormy owl!
Who for such maggots would not stoop?
Soup of the graveyard, horrible soup!
Soup of the graveyard, horrible soup!'

When I was younger, Tammy sometimes put joke eyeballs and big rubber insects in my bowl of soup, but I've mostly outgrown that now.

Later that night, we took the twins out to the baseball field in the middle of Regent Park. We all ran around until they were tired out and ready for sleep. We were all alone out there, just us. The air was clean and cold. Tammy and I played tag, and the twins ran with us. It felt great. It felt like we were the most powerful people in the world.

I could see other people looking down on us from their windows and their balconies. They could hear us laughing and having a good time. I wanted to wave to them all, so I did. Tammy saw what I was doing, and she laughed and waved, too. Some of the people waved back. I think our good time gave them a good time, too.

Back at home, I did my homework while Tammy put the boys to bed. When she didn't come back into the kitchen, I went into the boys' room. They have mattresses on the floor, like we have in the living room.

Mom was sound asleep, half of her on David's bed, half of her on the floor. It didn't surprise me to see her there. She often fell asleep when she was putting them to bed. She's almost always tired.

I covered Mom up with David's blanket and kissed her goodnight.

Our apartment has a tiny bedroom for Tammy and a bigger one for the twins. I have an alcove. It has a narrow bed built up high beside a window, with a ladder beside it. A curtain can be pulled across it, like the upper berth of a train. Underneath it is my bookshelf and a place to keep my clothes. My real treasures are on shelves by my bed. I keep the important stuff up high to keep my brothers out of it.

When I lie on my bunk and look out of the window, I sometimes pretend I'm on a train trip through the Gobi Desert, or in a bunk on a freighter ship, heading for the Cape of Storms.

This night, I didn't pretend to be anywhere but on the north-east corner of Regent Park, with my belly full of soup and my mom and little brothers asleep nearby.

It would be a while before I had such a good night again.

FOUR

THE CONSCIENCE OF
THE KING

'Are you sure you want to come?' I asked
Mom. 'It's a really dumb play. I look like
a fool in it.'

'Of course I want to come. It will make a
good story to embarrass you with to my grand-
children.' She buttoned David into his jacket.

Every year, in late October, my school holds
an open house to show the parents what their
miserable brats will be up to in the coming
year. Most of it's a lie, of course, but everyone
pretends it isn't. Last year, one of the parents
complained that his kid was in seventh grade
and still couldn't read, and what was the teacher
going to do about it? The teacher peered over
her glasses at him and asked him what was
wrong at home.

If the kid's a success, it's because of the school.
If the kid's a failure, it's because of the home.

Not all the teachers at my school are like that, just most of them. Good teachers don't want to teach at poor schools. People think poor kids are automatically failures, so why bother with us?

I'm not a failure. I've just turned eleven and I'm in grade eight. They bumped me ahead a couple of grades. Every year, though, the teachers warn Tammy that I'll come to a bad end. They think that because we're poor and my brothers are autistic and my mother used to be a stripper that I'm doomed to a life of crime and failure.

The eighth grade play is the highlight of the evening.

'If our play is the highlight, everyone's in for a big disappointment,' I grumbled as I buckled Daniel into his harness.

'"The play's the thing, wherein I'll catch the conscience of the king",' Tammy quoted. She used to do a dance to Elizabethan music. She quoted bits of Shakespeare while she was stripping. She said she enjoyed doing it, but the quotations went right over her audience's head. 'That's from *Hamlet*,' she said.

'Have you ever read the whole play?'

'Don't need to. That's the best line.'

'I thought the best line was "To be or not to be"?'

'Overrated.'

We keep the twins on harnesses when we're out walking with them. The harnesses keep them from running into the street. They don't understand about traffic.

I moaned and groaned some more about my part on the way over to the school.

'There are no dumb parts, just dumb players,' Tammy said.

'Oh, knock it off. Let me enjoy being grumpy.'

Tammy just laughed.

Tiffany, one of my classmates, and her gang of girls who follow her around like sheep were grouped just outside the school entrance.

They'll make good teenagers, I thought.

I headed for the backstage part of the auditorium. Mom was going to walk around with the twins until the play started. 'I'll try to tire them out so they'll sit through it,' she said.

The play was really dumb. It was written by a girl in our class who thought she was a great writer because teachers had told her so for years. They only told her that because she writes things they like.

In this play, a girl is nervous about starting grade eight. She has a dream the night before school starts, where a fairy godmother leads her through all the wonderful things she'll learn in the coming year. The girl wakes up in the morning looking forward to school. I was sure it would have the whole audience puking before it was halfway through.

I played an equilateral triangle. I wore a huge cardboard triangle around my neck, and I had one line. 'My sides are equal, and my corners are equal, so everything about me is equal.' Really deep.

Backstage, everything was chaos. Our teacher, Miss Melon—we called her the Watermelon or Melonball behind her back—was fluttering around, checking a million unimportant details. 'You'd think this was opening night on Broadway,' I mumbled. Before I could duck away, she spotted me.

'Good, you're finally here. Hurry and put on your costume.' She pushed me towards my fellow geometric shapes.

Tiffany and her gang arrived, and they were giggling as I walked past them towards the costume table.

'What's the joke?' I asked. 'I could use a laugh.'

'You're too young,' one of them said.

'Yeah, you wouldn't understand. You don't even wear a bra yet.'

'You don't think with your breasts, idiot,' I said back to them, 'or maybe you do.'

'Did you just call me an idiot?'

'What's the matter? Don't you understand what it means? Ask the Watermelon for a dictionary. Let me know if you need help with the alphabet.'

'You little . . .' Tiffany pushed me, hard, and I fell to the floor. My triangle got bent, which cheered me up considerably. I sprang up from the floor and started to push her back, when I felt a restraining hand on my shoulder.

The Watermelon had me in her grip. 'Khyber! Stop that! Look what you've done to your costume!'

'It looks better this way,' I muttered, although not loud enough for her to hear.

'Now, smarten up and no more nonsense. I'll put this down to backstage jitters, but if it happens again, you'll be in trouble.' Miss Melon didn't say anything to Tiffany. Tiffany's pretty. Adults never think pretty kids can do anything wrong.

I'm not pretty. I'm scrawny and my hair is always messy because I can't be bothered to comb it.

Tiffany had the starring role in the play, of course. She played the moronic girl who was afraid of grade eight. One of her gang members played the fairy godmother. They were strutting around backstage like a couple of peacocks. I felt kind of sorry for them. They didn't seem to realize what a joke the play was.

I watched the play from the side of the stage. It was as dopey as I'd remembered it from rehearsal. We were coming up to my entrance. I could hear the twins, way in the back. They were getting restless.

I entered the stage with the other shapes. Daniel was really starting to fuss, and as Tammy tried to calm him down, David slipped off his chair. He started walking around, touching other people and their things, making his special noises.

Good for you, David, I thought. Maybe there will be something fun about this evening after all. Daniel raised his noise level, too, adding to the fun. Tiffany had to raise her voice to be heard.

Then I saw the faces on the people in the

audience. They turned their heads, trying to show their disapproval of this woman who couldn't control her children. The people David touched withdrew from him like he had a bad smell.

'Why don't you put those dumb brothers of yours in a zoo, where they belong?' Tiffany growled at me.

That did it. I marched off the stage, adding to the twins' noise by stamping my feet. The play halted as I went down into the audience.

'Come with me, David,' I said. I picked him up. He put his warm little arms around my neck and let me carry him to the front of the auditorium. It was a bit hard going up the steps to the stage. David was getting heavy.

Up on stage, I glared at my classmates and at the audience. I belted out my stupid line, not knowing or caring whether it was my turn or not.

'My damn sides are equal, my damn corners are equal, so every damn thing about me is damn equal!'

I tore off my cardboard triangle, flung it to the floor, then stomped back off the stage.

Tammy and Daniel were waiting for me at the door. I got into my jacket, and we left the school.

'Come here, you,' Tammy said, once we were out in the cool night air.

She wrapped me in a huge hug. We put the boys between us, and we hugged them, too. It sure felt great.

I thought she'd bawl me out for swearing, but she didn't even mention it.

I went to bed happy that night, but I woke up a couple of hours later. I could hear Mom in the kitchen. She was crying.

I started to get out of my bed, but then I heard Juba's voice, soft and soothing. Juba is Mom's best friend. She lives in a tall apartment building at the other end of Regent Park.

Juba will take care of Mom, I thought, then drifted back to sleep.

FIVE

A WOMAN IN WHITE
TURNS RED

One of my friends is the waitress in the Trojan Horse Restaurant. She's the meanest waitress in Toronto.

That sounds rude, but it isn't. It's true. She was even written up in a magazine. They keep the article posted in the window. The owner says it's good for business. He says it quietly, though. He's a little afraid of her, even though he's her boss.

'I don't know how she's managed it, but she makes more than I do,' he whispered to me one Saturday when I was scrubbing pots. 'Plus, she gets tips!'

Her name is Valerie, and she must make a small fortune in tips. If she doesn't like the amount a customer has left, she'll call him back and make him leave more. I've even seen her run out of the restaurant after a customer.

'This is what you're leaving me?' she'll bark,

and usually the customer is so startled—and so scared—he'll cough up more money right then and there.

She only does that to rich people—well, people richer than us. There are rich people living all around the outside of Regent Park.

When people go into the Trojan Horse in need of a good meal but can't afford one, Valerie loads them up with extras of whatever they order. She's rude while she's doing it, though, like she's worried somebody might accuse her of being nice. Fat chance.

Valerie does have one weakness—babies. Whenever a baby comes into the Trojan Horse, she goes all gooey and gushy. The boss and I get a kick out of watching her. She'll take complete charge of the baby, and if the parent objects, or someone complains that she should put the baby down and get them their food, she growls at them like a dog protecting its bone. Parents who go to the Trojan Horse a lot wise up and let her take the baby, and then they enjoy a meal in peace. Babies never cry when Valerie is holding them. Maybe they feel how well she would protect them. Or maybe the sight of her mass of fiery red hair stuns them into silence.

Valerie is twice as grumpy after there's been a baby in the restaurant, to make up for being so gooey with the baby.

Valerie is rude with Tammy and me, too, but we're not afraid of her. She was Mom's friend before I was born. They met during Tammy's dancing days. Tammy would roll in for breakfast at two in the afternoon, three hours after the breakfast menu had ended. Valerie would growl at her, and Tammy would growl right back, so naturally they became good friends.

Valerie was gooey with me for the first year of my life, bringing me a teddy bear the day I was born. I still have it. She was Mom's labour coach, too. She practically ordered Mom to hurry up and give birth and stop fooling around.

She stopped being gooey with me and started being grumpy when I was about a year old. I grew up with her rudeness. I like it. When I'm an adult, I'm going to be just as rude as Valerie. I just wish Tammy would let me practise more now.

Valerie's crazy about the boys. I like people who like my brothers. She's rude to them, too, but they seem to know when they're safe and around friends. If anyone in the restaurant complains about the twins' noises or arm-flapping, she takes their food away and tells them to leave. I love it when she does that.

I work at the Trojan Horse for one hour every Saturday morning. It's not a real job, since I'm too young, but it's still a job. Valerie got it for me. She told the boss that this was the way it was going to be. The boss nodded meekly and disappeared behind the grill.

I love arriving at the restaurant. It smells of bacon and stale cigarette smoke, grease and old coffee. It's warm and cheerful.

'Quit blocking the door,' Valerie snarled when I got to work that morning. I grinned at her and hurried to hang up my jacket.

'Here, clean this!' Valerie pointed to something greasy and gross. She usually has me clean something like that.

'Ugh. Did you save this up for me all week?'

'Less talk and more work!'

I shut up and got to work.

When whatever it was was finally clean, my hour was up. I sat down at the back table, the one reserved for the employees, and Valerie brought me my breakfast. I get breakfast in exchange for work. Having breakfast in a restaurant is great. It makes me feel like a big shot.

I got the Saturday papers from behind the counter, smothered my eggs in ketchup, making them look bloody and messy, and settled down to eat. Valerie gives me extra bacon. I like to dip it in the egg yolk.

After breakfast I spent some time at the library, and by then it was time for lunch.

Tammy had chores for me, as always, then David and I walked over to Allan Gardens. We ran outside for a while, then went into the greenhouse to wait for a wedding.

Working a wedding was my secret job. Secret from Tammy, that is. She never expressly said I couldn't do it, but only because she never imagined that I would.

David, of course, would never tell. Sometimes it's useful to have autistic brothers.

David and I sat on the centre bench in the greenhouse, the most popular bench for weddings. I gave David a couple of buttons to play with so he wouldn't be bored.

We didn't have to wait long.

A wedding party swarmed into the greenhouse and headed for my bench. Their faces dropped when they saw David and me sitting on that bench like we owned it.

'Hello.' The photographer nodded to me, all friendly. I recognized the style. It didn't throw me a bit. Before I got through with him, he'd be tearing out what was left of his hair.

I nodded hello back, to put him off his guard. He got busy setting up his camera. It was pointed at my bench. He, and everyone else, assumed I would move. As he busied himself with the light meter and other gadgets, the wedding party looked at David and me. They tried to smile pleasantly, because they could see David was special, and they didn't want anybody to accuse them of being mean to special children. Everything was proceeding as it should.

'Now, if I could just ask this pretty young lady to step off to the side for a few moments . . .' The photographer smiled at me again.

I smiled back. I didn't move.

The best man came on to the scene. 'Are we ready?'

The photographer glanced in my direction. The best man (if he was their best man, I'd hate to see their worst one) nodded, as if he knew his duty and would do it. He sauntered over to me, with all the time in the world. He sat his ugly self down beside me.

'What have you got there, sport?' he asked David. 'Some buttons?'

David made one of his noises and kept playing with his buttons.

The best man tried me next. 'We're hoping to take some pictures here. You don't mind, do you?'

'No, I don't mind.'

'Good.' He got off the bench, feeling victorious. 'You just have to know how to talk to them,' he said to the photographer.

I still didn't move.

The best man came back to me and said, 'Uh, the thing is, we'd like to use the bench.'

'Go right ahead.'

'Well, we'd like you to move.'

I didn't.

The best man looked helplessly at the groom. The groom was even uglier than the best man.

The groom dug into the pocket of his tuxedo and pulled out a two-dollar coin. 'Here you are. Go buy yourself some candy.'

'Thank you,' I said. I stayed where I was.

'What's the hold-up here?' The bride rushed up to the gang around the bench. The rest of the wedding party crowded around.

'Look, little girl, we'd like to take some photographs here, and you're in our way, so would you please move?'

I sat still.

'She must be retarded,' the bride said to the men. 'This is my wedding day,' she said to me, very loudly and slowly. 'Do you understand? My wedding day?'

I stared right back at her.

'Give the brat some more money,' she snapped at the groom. He handed me another two-dollar coin, and was about to put his change back in his pocket when the bride grabbed it all out of his hand and practically threw it at me.

'Buy some candy for your brother, too,' he said. I thanked him. I didn't thank the bride.

'We've asked you nicely. Now will you get out of here?'

I blinked, the picture of innocence. David turned the volume up on his noise, and started jumping and flapping his arms.

Next came my favourite part. Someone always lost their temper, and I always enjoyed it. When Tammy loses her temper at me, I hate it, but when strangers do, particularly when I haven't done anything wrong, I enjoy it immensely.

This time, it was the bride. Her face got red and her cheeks puffed out, and she started sounding like a pot about to boil over. I didn't like her. I didn't like any of them. Sometimes I do, and I leave quite pleasantly after the first bribe, but I didn't like these people. The bride's dress must have cost more than Mom spends on rent in a whole year, maybe five years, even.

'Listen, kid, I've spent a long time planning for this day, and so far, everything has been perfect, and I am not going to let you ruin it!' Her voice screeched like the crows and gulls that hang around the garbage bin. She was as ugly as the groom. In fact, everyone in the wedding party was ugly. You'd think that, with all that money, they'd invest in plastic surgery.

'Get off that bench and take your defective brother with you, before I throw you off myself!' The Bride of Frankenstein was spitting, she was so angry.

I usually don't make nasty comments when I'm working a wedding, but because she insulted my brother, I let one fly.

'Your bridesmaids' dresses are the colour of puke,' I said.

The bridesmaids looked at themselves, and I

saw from their faces that they realized I was right. Even if they liked the dresses before, they never would again.

Happy to have the last word, I took David's hand, and we walked calmly out of the greenhouse.

I liked having money in my pocket. I was saving for something big, so I couldn't spend much of it, but I splurged and bought some gummi feet for David and me. I knew that eating gummi feet wouldn't really increase my chances of becoming an explorer of faraway places, but it couldn't hurt, either.

SIX

TROUBLED WATERS

We went to church Sunday morning, as usual. The twins went to the nursery, I went to Sunday school, and Mom got a quiet hour without kids.

I haven't decided about God, but I do like Sunday school. My class was small, and the teacher and I spent a lot of time looking at an old atlas of the Bible, and talking about camels. I know a lot about camels.

'The weather doesn't look very good,' Tammy said, as we were walking home.

'Oh, Mom, it's all right, and anyway, you promised!'

Tammy laughed at my pleading face. 'OK, stop begging. We'll go.'

Tammy had been saying for weeks that we would go to the Toronto Islands one Sunday, and had put aside enough money for the ferry tickets. We would have to walk to the ferry, which is a

DEBORAH ELLIS

42

long way from Regent Park, but that was fine with me, since we would go down Yonge Street.

Yonge Street is Toronto's busiest street. Tammy didn't allow me to go there on my own, because of the rough people who hang out there.

On the way, I dragged Tammy into the army surplus store. I dragged her in there every time we went to Yonge Street.

'Not again, Khyber,' she protested. 'All that canvas and camping equipment. Why don't we go try on dresses instead?' She was kidding me. She knew I'd rather spend an hour with Miss Melon than ten minutes trying on dresses.

The greatest backpack in the world was in the army surplus store. I'd been looking at it for months. It cost sixty dollars. Although I had fourteen dollars saved, I'd have to work a lot more weddings before I could buy it.

'This is the one?' Tammy asked, lifting it down off the wall hook so I could hold it. The twins were restless, so I knew I'd only have a moment with it.

'This is it,' I replied. It had lots of pockets, including secret pockets, deep inside the pack. I showed them to Tammy. 'I could do some great exploring with this!'

'You certainly could,' Tammy said, putting it back. 'Maybe one day we can get it for you.' David started screeching, so we had to leave without looking at all the gadgets in the glass cases, but at least I got to see the pack.

Tammy didn't know about the wedding money, of course. I kept it in a little bag under my mattress.

All the way down to the lake I yakked about the backpack and what I'd put in each pocket. Tammy probably wasn't listening—even though the boys were on their harnesses, it still takes a lot of work to move them through the crowds— but I didn't care. I was happy to have her within hearing range of my voice.

It was cold on the ferry, but we stood on the upper deck, enjoying the fresh wind on our faces.

'Happy,' said David.

'You feel happy. That's very good talking, David,' Mom said. It was important to encourage the boys every time they said something or made eye contact. Mom spent an hour a day with each of them, trying to get them to talk or look her in the eye. Each time they did, they got a little piece of marshmallow. It was a programme Tammy had read about in one of her autism books. She taught me to do it, too.

For a while I couldn't understand what the big deal was about eye contact. Then Tammy spent a whole day without making eye contact with me. After that, I understood.

'The boys are growing fast,' Tammy said.

'They're getting heavy, too.'

'They take after their father,' Tammy said. 'He was tall. Do you remember?'

'How could I forget. He was ugly, too. But the boys aren't ugly.'

'No, they're very handsome.'

'We should try to get them in the movies. I hear they use a lot of twins when they're making movies. Would you like that, Daniel? Would you like to be a movie star?' Daniel hooted and jumped up and down, but he does that all the time, anyway, so I had no way of knowing if he was agreeing with me.

We landed at Ward's Island and walked around there for a while, looking at the little houses, picking out the ones we'd like to live in. Then we walked along the boardwalk beside the lake to Centre Island, where the amusement park was. It was shut down for the season, but I liked it better then. Besides, we never had money to go on any of the rides when they were open.

Centreville had a closed-up look, like its body was there but its spirit was some place else.

'Centreville is like the twins,' I said to Tammy.

'What do you mean?'

'Well, we know there's something great inside those boarded-up places, but we just don't know how to get to it.'

Tammy put a hand on my head to show she liked what I said. 'Your ears are cold. I should have made you wear a hat.' She pulled the boys' hats down lower over their ears. 'We should head back soon.'

'What about the picnic?'

We sat on a bench outside the Haunted Barrel Factory, had our sandwiches and made up names for other scary rides.

'How about the Haunted Beauty Parlour,' Tammy suggested. 'When you come out of it you've got a bad perm.'

'Or the Haunted Subway Tunnel. That would be a good one. You'd get on this subway car and go through a tunnel full of ghosts and body parts.'

'How about a Haunted Welfare Office?'

'With social workers all over the place! No,

that would be too scary. How about a Haunted Eighth Grade Homeroom? Miss Melon could be there, as herself!'

'You've got Miss Melon on the brain.'

'Melon brain—ha-ha!'

We arrived at the Centre Island ferry docks just as the ferry was pulling away.

'Let's walk back to Ward's and catch the ferry there,' Mom said. 'The walk will keep us warm.'

We trudged back towards Ward's Island. 'The boys will sleep tonight with all this exercise and fresh air,' I said. 'Sometimes it seems like everything we do with the twins during the day is to help them sleep at night.'

We walked through Far Enough Farm again. 'We'd better not stop this time,' Mom said. 'I don't like the look of that sky.' We had to stop a little bit, though. We were the only people at the farm. The animals were probably lonely.

'Khyber,' Mom began, 'there's something important I have to talk to you about.'

'What?'

'It's about the boys. They are beginning to need more care than we can give them. They need to go to school. They need to go to a special school.'

This was important, all right, but I didn't understand what the big deal was, unless she wanted me to take them there every morning and pick them up every afternoon. 'Is the school near our place? Can they walk there?'

'No, the school is not near our place. There are no schools for autistic children near our place.'

'They'll have to take a streetcar, then. They won't like that during rush hour, but maybe the school will teach them not to mind it.'

'It's not just the school, it's . . . I don't know how to say this to you. The boys need to be someplace where there are trained people to look after them.'

'Look after them?'

'I just can't do it any more. Maybe if I were not on my own . . .'

'You're not on your own. You have me.'

'But you're not an adult, and even if you were, I wouldn't expect you to spend your life caring for your brothers. I wouldn't let you.'

'I don't understand what you're saying.'

'What I'm saying is this.' Mom took a deep breath. 'I've found a group home that will take Daniel and David. It's out in the country. They have a school on the grounds, and some animals, and they'll take both boys. I won't have to split them up.'

'A group home? You mean they're not going to live with us any more?'

'Think of it as a boarding school, darling.'

I clutched Daniel's hand more tightly. 'No. I don't want them to go.'

'Neither do I, but we've got to think about what's best for them. They need people taking care of them who have energy, who have skills. I have neither of those things.'

'So you're just going to give them away.'

'Don't overdramatize. I'm not giving them away. Boy, Khyber, you know just what to say to get me mad!'

'Maybe you should give me away, too, as long as you're handing out children. In fact, why give them away? Why not sell them? You can use the money to buy more Monkees records.'

Tammy took the boys' hands and walked away from me.

I followed her, saying nasty, vile things all the way across Ward's Island.

'You're probably doing this so you can become a stripper again,' I said. 'First you put your sons in a home, then you'll put me in a home, then you'll have the apartment all to yourself. You'll sell us, then you'll have lots of other children, and you'll sell them, too.'

All the way to the ferry docks, I kept it up. Tammy didn't say a word. If Tammy had been a hitting kind of a mother, I would have been hit a thousand times. Tammy's never hit me or the boys, though. I don't think she knows how.

Rain started to come down, first in light spats, then it really started to pour. We ran, but we were still pretty wet by the time we reached the small shelter near the ferry docks.

Inside the shelter, Mom spoke. 'This is not your decision to make, Khyber. This is mine. David and Daniel need to be around people who are trained, who can teach them.'

I listened to the rain pattering down around us.

'Khyber, I'm tired. I just can't do it any more. I'm not able to give the boys what they need, and I'm not able to give you what you need. Every cent we have goes to treatment for the boys, and none of those treatments have helped one bit. All those people with brilliant ideas who take advantage of someone like me . . .' Tammy started to cry, but stopped herself.

'Maybe I've been wrong in not talking to you about this before,' Tammy said. 'It wouldn't have come as such a shock. I've been trying to get them into a home for some time.'

I stood up. 'I thought they were in a home,' I said, and stomped out into the rain.

Living without my brothers? Not tucking them into bed at night, all warm from their baths? Not taking them out every day after school? Not dancing with them to Tammy's Monkees records? Singing the soup song without them there?

By the time the ferry came, I was soaked through to the skin. My teeth were chattering. I didn't try to stop shivering. I wanted Tammy to feel guilty for making me get cold and wet.

We sat in the downstairs part of the ferry. I grabbed David's and Daniel's hands and took them to a seat a fair bit away from Tammy. The boys will usually go with me anywhere, but they must have felt my anger. They screamed and yanked themselves away from me—they were growing strong as well as tall and heavy—and stood off by themselves.

The walk home was long and cold, and by the time we got there, we were all chilled and miserable. Tammy tossed the boys in a hot bath, while I got out of my wet clothes and into my robe. The soup was hot by the time I finished my bath.

I didn't sing the soup song. Tammy didn't deserve it.

SEVEN

IN THE MIDDLE OF
THE NIGHT

Mom kept me home from school Monday
because I caught a cold in the rain. She
was gone practically all day with the twins.
She didn't tell me where she was going.

I spent most of the day on my bunk, reading
and studying for the history test we were having
the next day. Outside, the world was grey and
drizzly. It was nice to be in my bed with a book
and a bowl of soup. I wondered where X was. I
hoped she was warm and dry.

When Mom came back with my brothers,
she wouldn't answer any of my questions, and I
soon got tired of asking. I was still mad at her.

I used my cold as an excuse to go to bed early.
I didn't lift a finger to help her with the twins.

Maybe because I'd been dozing on and off all
day, it took me a while to get to sleep that night.
When I finally did, I was woken up by something

patting me in the face. I must have been dreaming, because it scared me, and I slapped out at whatever it was.

I heard a thud, and then a scream, and then I was wide awake.

Daniel was lying on the floor below my bunk.

'Mom! Mom, get up! Daniel's hurt!' Mom was right there even before I finished yelling for her.

There was blood pouring from a gash on Daniel's head. He was screaming from the pain and fear. David woke up, and he started screaming, too.

'I'll call an ambulance,' I said, and ran to the phone. I punched in 911, but there was no sound. I had forgotten that our phone had been cut off. Tammy had spent the phone money on special vitamins for the boys.

'Get your coat on, Khyber, and get David's on, too.'

'But . . .'

'Now!' Tammy was throwing her own coat on over her nightgown. She grabbed my blanket to wrap Daniel in. 'Put your boots on, too.'

I scrambled to get ready. David didn't want to go out. He plopped down on the floor and kept kicking his boots off and screaming. Mom couldn't help me. She was busy with Daniel.

'Grab him and let's go!' she said.

I lifted him up and carried him out of the door. He kicked his boots off, but I just let them stay there on the hall floor. I couldn't have carried them anyway. David was heavy enough when he was co-operating. When he was screaming in my ear and hitting me and kicking me, I could barely keep from dropping him.

'Can't I stay home with David?' I asked.

'I'm not leaving you alone here at night. It's too dangerous. Now, come on.'

Some of the neighbours opened their doors as we walked past. They were mad at having been woken up.

'Lady, can't you shut those kids up?' said one.

'Some people shouldn't be allowed to have kids,' said another. I was too busy with David to yell back at them.

'There's a cab!' I told Tammy, seeing the taxi's lit sign heading towards us on Gerrard.

'Come on, Khyber, let's catch this light.'

'Are we taking a streetcar?' The streetcar going west on Gerrard would take us close to the Sick Kids Hospital.

Tammy didn't answer me. She kept going past the streetcar stop.

'Hurry up!' she ordered, then darted out across Parliament Street between two parked cars, something she had told me never to do.

'I can't keep going,' I said. David kept hitting me in the head and screaming next to my ear. My jacket hadn't completely dried out from Sunday, and it was cold and clammy next to my nightgown. To make things even worse, I'd been in such a hurry, I'd put my boots on the wrong feet.

'Mom!'

'Khyber, shut up! I've got enough to worry about without you complaining. Next time, keep your hands to yourself.'

That shocked me. 'This wasn't my fault!'

'Well, it certainly wasn't mine!'

How could Mom think that I would hurt Daniel on purpose? My disbelief and shame kept me quiet the rest of the way to the hospital.

The closest hospital to Regent Park is a few blocks north and a few blocks west. As we hurried there, we woke up all the street people sleeping in doorways. We must have been quite a sight.

The waiting room at the emergency department was full. It always is when we have to take one of the boys in. Usually we go to the Sick Kids Hospital, but that's a long way to have to walk.

'Where are David's boots?' Mom asked, as we waited in line to see the admitting nurse. The boys kept screaming. At least we didn't have to ring the desk bell to let the nurse know we were there.

'They fell off in the hall,' I said.

'They'd better be there when we get back.'

'What are you mad at me for? He kicked them off!'

'Take David into the waiting room and get him quiet,' Tammy told me, 'and don't let him run around in his bare feet. The floor is wet and cold and I don't want him getting sick, although you've probably already given him your cold.'

I did as I was told. At least, I took David into the waiting room. I couldn't make him quiet, though, and between him and his brother, the screaming sounded like it was on stereo speakers. The other people in the waiting room were not pleased with us. On top of everything else, David's nappy needed changing.

There were two empty seats next to each other. I sat down in one and put David in the other, but he wouldn't stay in it. He kept sliding to the floor and kneeling into his rocking and head-banging position. Tammy was right—the floor was wet. There was an old man near us who smelled even worse than David did. He had wet himself, too. I couldn't tell if the floor was wet from the rain or from him.

I was angry and tired, my nose was stuffed up, and I was chilled from my cold and my wet jacket. My arms were sore from carrying David, I was tired of his screams, and my scalp hurt where he had pulled on my hair. Because I felt so lousy, I was rough with him, pulling him back into his chair when he slid out of it, and telling him to shut up. My impatience only made him worse. The boys can understand other people's emotions even if they can't understand words. To get David quiet, I'd have to be calm and friendly. I didn't feel calm and friendly.

Tammy didn't make anything better when she and Daniel joined us in the waiting room. She had been given a towel to hold to his head, but he was still screaming.

'He got blood on my blanket,' I said.

'It will wash out,' Mom said.

'Blood doesn't wash out.'

'He couldn't help it.'

'But it's my blanket! Why didn't you wrap him in one of your blankets? Why did you have to use my blanket?' I knew I was acting like a jerk, but I didn't feel like acting like anything else.

In other circumstances, this would have been an adventure, being out in the middle of the night. There were lots of strange-looking people in the waiting room. I could have imagined that their wounds had come from exciting battles, and their sicknesses were rare, tropical diseases they'd got while searching for lost treasure. But you have to be in a good mood to imagine things.

EIGHT

FIGHT

The night had turned into day by the time we got home.

'Can't we take a taxi?' I pleaded.

'There's no money for a taxi,' Tammy replied, 'and there's no money for a streetcar, either, so don't bother to ask.'

We walked back.

David would have walked, but since he was in his bare feet, I had to carry him. Tammy carried Daniel, whose hair had been partly shaved off to make room for a big white bandage. He'd been given stitches. Mom had to be there with him while they did it, to help the doctors hold him down. She said they had frozen the area around the cut, so he didn't feel any pain, but he screamed and fought them anyway.

Both boys hate having their hair washed or cut. Daniel would have really hated having all those people around him, doing things to his face.

Daniel was asleep in Tammy's arms, which made him a lot easier to carry than David. David wanted to walk, so he squirmed and fought me all the way home. I wanted to ask Tammy if we could trade boys, but she looked angry at me still, so I didn't ask.

David's boots were still in the hallway, and I kicked them into the apartment ahead of me. I was glad to put him down, and I think he was glad to get away from me, too. I crawled up to my bunk, remembering too late that Tammy had my blanket, and it was covered with blood.

Mom put the twins in their room, then helped me off with my jacket. I was too tired to do it myself. She got me into a dry nightgown, then covered me up with her own bedspread.

'I didn't do it on purpose,' I said.

'I know you didn't. But do you see what I mean, about the boys being too much for us?'

I rolled over in the bunk, turning my back to her. She kissed me goodnight anyway.

The alarm clock went off a couple of hours later. Tammy wanted me to stay home from school again, but we were having a history test, so I stumbled, bleary-eyed, into the classroom.

I walked into class in the middle of the national

anthem, which was a crime on two counts. I was late, and we were supposed to stand still, at attention, and sing when 'O Canada' was on.

'We'll see you in detention this afternoon,' Miss Melon told me, as soon as the last 'We stand on guard for thee' had been sung.

The test was first thing in the morning. That's one decent thing about Miss Melon. She gets the nasty stuff out of the way early, so we don't have to sit and stew about it all day. All tests are first thing in the morning. She says our brains are fresher then, and she gets a truer picture of how empty our heads are. If Miss Melon ever said anything nice she'd probably have a stroke.

The history test was about the building of the national railway. History is usually pretty interesting, since it's full of explorers and adventures. I knew the answers to the test questions, but somewhere between writing my name at the top of the paper and morning recess, I fell asleep.

'Here's one test paper I can mark in a hurry,' Melonball said, picking up my paper and waving it at the class. Everyone laughed. Everyone but me.

Out in the school yard, things got worse. We were barely five minutes into recess when trouble started.

Tiffany and her gang were in the school yard already. They started yelling insults at me as soon as they saw me walk out of the building.

'Hey, Sunken Chest! You finally had the guts to show up!' They call me Sunken Chest because I'm flat-chested. It's supposed to hurt my feelings.

'She thinks she can just ruin the class play and get away with it.'

'Who does she think she is?'

'What kind of a name is Khyber? We should call her Creeper. Hey, Creeper, do you like your new name?'

'She's probably on drugs. That's why she keeps falling asleep in class.'

I kept walking away from them. They followed me. I walked to the far end of the playground, but they kept walking behind me.

In her dancing days, when people in the audience got on her nerves, Mom pretended they were cattle. I pretended I was being followed by a herd of big, dumb cows. I could almost hear them moo.

I'm leading them to the barn, I thought. I'll put them in the barn, close the door, lock them in, and not let them out until I feel like it.

It worked until we got to the fence. I pressed my tummy against it and hooked my fingers into the wires. The herd of angry girls pressed in around me. The world outside the school yard looked far away.

They started poking at me.

Ring, bell, ring, will you? I almost said my plea out loud. Tammy didn't like me fighting. If I could hold my temper for just a few more minutes, the bell would ring, and the gang would leave me alone for a while.

Then Tiffany spoke up. 'Look, here come Creeper's little brothers.'

Tammy was coming! She'd get me out of this. I looked eagerly towards where Tiffany was pointing.

She was pointing at a woman walking two little dogs.

The other girls started laughing and making barking sounds. I turned and looked at Tiffany. She smiled a mean smile.

In an instant, she was on the ground with me on top of her. She was bigger than me, but I was angrier. Besides, the only exercise Tiffany ever got was brushing her hair.

'How dare you insult my brothers!' I yelled. It felt good to punch her. It felt like I was not just fighting her, I was fighting the audience at the play, all the social workers who ever made Tammy feel bad, and everyone on the street who had ever made a sour face around my brothers. That's a lot of fighting.

The kids in the playground formed a ring around us, chanting, 'Fight! Fight! Fight!' Tiffany was punching back, pulling my hair and scratching me with her sharp nails. For a minute she was on top of me, pounding my chest. I had just got back on top of her when the teachers broke through the tight ring of kids and pulled me off her.

I kept swinging. I landed a fist in Miss Melon's stomach, but only because it was in the way. I felt bad about that later, when I'd calmed down. I didn't like Miss Melon, but I had no reason to hit her. That was the only part of the fight I felt bad about.

It took a whole army of teachers to hold me down and get me into the school. Out of the corner of my eye, I could see Tiffany being gently helped to her feet. She leaned against the vice-principal, limping and crying. Her hair was a mess.

They stuck me in one of the little guidance offices and locked the door. I banged around in there for a while, throwing the chairs against the walls, until I got tired. I was bleeding from being scratched by Tiffany's nails, and my chest hurt, but the nurse didn't come to see me.

After a while, they opened the door and let me out.

Mom was there. 'Hasn't this child seen a nurse?'

'The nurse is busy with young Tiffany,' the vice-principal said.

'What's the matter with the rest of you? Don't you know how to open a bandage? Get me your first-aid kit.'

No one moved. Tammy banged her way behind the office counter. 'Get me a first-aid kit right now,' she said into the vice-principal's face. She used her quiet voice. I knew that voice. It was her don't-even-think-about-messing-with-me voice.

'Get her the first-aid kit,' he said to one of the secretaries. He tried to make it sound like it was all his idea. It was kind of funny.

Tammy grabbed the kit without saying thank you. Then she grabbed me and headed out of the office.

'Wait a minute,' Miss Melon said. 'I don't think you understand the seriousness . . .'

'Clean up first, lecture second,' Mom said, and pulled me through the office door.

I was impressed with the sight of myself in the cloakroom mirror. Tiffany had put deep scratches on my head. My face was covered with streams of dried blood. I looked wonderfully gory.

Tammy wet some paper towels and started cleaning me up.

'I've told you and told you and told you that I don't want you fighting.' She bandaged the worst cuts and tidied my hair. 'Are you hurt anywhere else?'

I told her about my chest. She felt me all over and said she thought I was in one piece.

'All right, now, quickly, before we go back to the office. What happened?'

I thought about telling her the truth, but if she knew I was fighting because of the boys, she might send them away faster. I looked at a piece of chewed-up pink gum on the cloakroom floor and mumbled, 'She just annoyed me, that's all.'

'She annoyed you.'

I don't like lying to Tammy. I hardly ever do it. When I have to lie, I make my lies as true as possible. Tiffany had annoyed me, so it was partly true.

Tammy always sticks up for me with the teachers. She'll bawl me out when we're alone, but never in front of anybody. Some parents like to suck up to the teachers by yelling at their kids in front of them. They think the teachers will think they're good parents if they do that. Tammy doesn't care what teachers think of her.

We went back to the principal's office. Everyone was looking very solemn and stern. Tiffany's mother was there. Tiffany was still in the nurse's office, probably having over-acted hysterics.

I sat through a long list of complaints about my behaviour.

When they ran out of complaints about my attitude and temper, Miss Melon piped up, 'Plus, she was late again this morning, and she fell asleep during the history test.'

'She fell asleep during the history test because she was up all night in the hospital emergency room with her brothers,' Tammy replied. The other adults looked uncomfortable for a moment and stared down at the floor, embarrassed.

The vice-principal recovered first. 'She can be excused for being late and falling asleep, but she cannot be excused for fighting.'

I stopped listening at that point.

While the adults went on and on about my crime, and Tammy reminded them that I was the brightest kid in the school, and it was their job to give me confidence instead of making me feel bad, I pretended I was far away, crossing the Australian Outback, all on my own.

They suspended me for the rest of the week and I'd be on probation when I returned, plus I'd have to apologize to Tiffany. Before we could leave, we had to go back to the classroom and get the school work that I would miss.

'Whatever she gives you, I will double it,' Mom said, bending down close to my ear so that no one else would hear her.

We didn't talk on the way home. Tammy was unhappy with me, especially since she didn't know the real reason I'd been fighting.

I wasn't unhappy with me, though. Anybody insults my brothers, they're going to get it.

'You could at least pretend to be ashamed of yourself,' Tammy said. I did not reply.

Mom had to get back to the boys at the play group, but before she left, she wrote down a list of chores for me to get started on. 'I'll give you more work this afternoon. You won't have a moment to breathe until you go back to school.'

Then she put her face close to mine and said in her quiet, don't-mess-with-me voice, 'I absolutely forbid you to fight. Do you understand?'

I nodded. There were very few things Tammy forbade me to do, but when she did, there was no discussion. That was Law. I'd never disobeyed her on anything she absolutely forbade me to do.

Mom left. I looked at the long list of chores, and got started.

NINE

EXILE

Mom was, as always, true to her word. When I wasn't cleaning, I was running errands, and when she ran out of chores for me to do at our place, she sent me over to Juba's to clean stuff there. When I wasn't cleaning, I was doing school work.

Tammy didn't just double my homework, she tripled it. For every page of maths the teacher gave me, Mom gave me two more. She gave me long columns of numbers to add up, my least favourite kind of arithmetic. She made me read ahead in history and do pages and pages of grammar.

For someone like me, who hates work, it was a bleak week.

'Don't even think about complaining,' Tammy warned me when she handed me the first list of chores I was to complete.

I hadn't thought of complaining. I'd learned

from painful experience that complaining about a punishment only brought on more punishment. Besides, Tammy says that one way a person's character can be measured is by how well she takes her punishment, if it's deserved. It's funny but no matter how mad I get at Tammy, I still want her to think I'm a person of good character.

Mom always told me there's no shame in being punished for something you did wrong, but there is shame in whining about it. It helped this time that I knew I did the right thing, clobbering Tiffany. Fighting is wrong, but I was still glad I did it.

When I wasn't busy with housework or school work, I had to take the twins out, one at a time, one hour each brother, morning and afternoon.

'You're confined to the playground behind the building,' Tammy said. 'You can go there, and nowhere else.'

I hated taking the twins to that playground. It was small, with just a jungle-gym in a sandpit. There was no fence around it, and it was right next to a parking lot, so I was always afraid they would get hit by a car. I love my brothers, but spending four hours a day with them in that tiny playground got a little boring.

The week dragged on. 'No radio, no books except school books,' Tammy decreed.

'What about Monkees records?' I asked.

She didn't think that was funny.

I even had to turn over my atlases to her.

Then, finally, it was over. Friday night appeared.

Just before going to bed, I went into the kitchen, where Juba and Mom were having a cup of tea. Since they've known each other, Juba and Mom must have drunk an ocean of tea at that table. Sometimes they go to Juba's, but with the boys, it's easier when Juba comes to our place. Besides, Juba's apartment is really tiny. She likes to get out of it as much as she can, she says, so the walls don't close in on her.

Juba used to babysit me when I was too young and stupid to look after myself. She was a thousand years old then, and must be almost two thousand years old now, but she has a soft lap, one that's almost as good as Tammy's. When I was little and had a fight with Tammy, I'd go crying to Juba. She'd take me on to her lap, rock me, let me cry it out, then dry my tears and say, 'It's time for you to bring a little sunshine into the world.' It sounds crazy, but by the time she said that, I wouldn't be mad at Mom any more.

All my friends are dependable. Juba is always kind, Valerie is always rude, and X is always frightened.

I put my stack of homework down in front of Tammy. 'All done. Spelling checked, maths checked, everything checked.'

Mom thumbed through the pages of school work. 'This looks nice and neat.'

As if I'd waste my time bringing her school-work that wasn't tidy.

'Let's hear the poem.'

For extra English homework, Tammy gave me a poem to learn out of a big book of poetry she found at the Goodwill years ago. Memorizing stuff is easy. You just say it over and over until it becomes as much a part of you as your name.

I've learned a lot of poetry over the years. Lewis Carroll is my overall favourite. Tammy would find a new poem for me to learn whenever I got in her hair. She said she'd do anything that would keep me quiet for more than two minutes at a time.

I talk a lot because I have a lot to say. People who don't talk a lot also might have a lot to say. They just don't know how to get to it.

What I hate most are people who talk a lot and have nothing to say. They think they have a lot to say, so they keep talking and talking, but when you listen to them, they really aren't saying anything.

The poem Tammy gave me to learn during my punishment week was called 'The Buried Life' by Matthew Arnold. That's what I was living that week—a buried life, buried in work.

The poem is a long one, with twenty verses. It's about how we live on the surface of ourselves, and rarely get a chance to know what we're really made of. The day-to-day junk of work or school and chores and doing what you're supposed to do to be a good citizen doesn't leave much time to find out how to be a good human being.

My favourite verse goes like this:

But often, in the world's most crowded streets,
But often, in the din of strife,
There rises an unspeakable desire
After the knowledge of our buried life.

I think it means that in the middle of being busy doing stuff, you can suddenly wonder, 'Who am I? What am I doing here?' I'm glad somebody put that into a poem, because it's happened to me. I guess everybody loses track of where they are sometimes.

I recited the poem, and I recited it correctly, and when I was done, Tammy said, 'Once more, with feeling,' which is an old joke of ours, so I knew I was out of the dog house.

'Can I have my atlases back?'

'Well, I should make you wait until I've had time to make sure your school work is correct.'

I held my breath. Juba and Tammy laughed at the expression on my face. Tammy went into her room to get my atlases.

Mom's room is different from the rest of the apartment. 'I must have one haven of femininity in this apartment filled with boys and explorers!' she says. The room is all pink and yellow, with lots of dainty things she's picked up at the Goodwill and yard sales over the years. It's a pretty room, although I wouldn't like to have one like it.

In her closet, she keeps some of her costumes from when she was a dancer. I used to play dressing-up with them when I was a little kid. Now that I'm too old to dress up myself, I sometimes dress up the boys. Tammy's old costumes are great dressing-up clothes—feather boas, capes, sparkly things. It's hard to imagine Tammy even wearing that stuff. These days, she wears only jeans and sweaters. She dresses like me, only tidier.

I don't go into Tammy's room without her permission (unless I need her during the night) and she doesn't go into my alcove. I don't mess with her stuff unless she says it's OK, and she doesn't mess with mine. One of the main reasons I won't do drugs is that Tammy says any hint of me smoking dope means she gets to 'plough through my stuff like there's no tomorrow'. I like my privacy.

Tammy handed me my atlases, and I crawled into bed with them. I have three atlases now—a Canadian atlas, a little kid's atlas that I keep because it has photographs in it of faraway places, and a thick world atlas. They're a little out of date—we bought them at the Goodwill—but I still love them.

I plotted a journey across Egypt, following the Nile River from the Mediterranean Sea to Lake Nasser, until it was time to go to sleep.

Tammy came in to kiss me goodnight.

'I'm proud of you,' she said. 'It was a long, hard week for you, and you came through it really well.'

'Can we do something tomorrow? All of us? Could we go to Riverdale Farm?' Riverdale Farm is a real farm, with pigs and horses and chickens, a few blocks from our place. Tammy lets me go there alone, but it's more fun to go with my whole family.

Tammy hesitated. Then she said, 'As a matter of fact, we can do something. We can go see the boys' new home tomorrow.'

I sat up on my elbows. 'What?'

'The social worker will be by in the morning to drive us there. We'll be spending the night there, to help get the boys used to it. I was going to leave you with Juba, but I'd much rather you came with us.'

'You're still doing that? I said I didn't want you to.' I sat all the way up. My head bumped the ceiling. If I grew any more, we'd have to get a taller apartment.

'Lower your voice, young lady. If you wake up your brothers, you'll be the one sitting up with them all night.'

'You're still giving them away?'

Tammy turned off my light. 'Go to sleep, Khyber. I'd love to have you come with us tomorrow, but if you don't want to, you can go to Juba's after your job. We won't be back until late Sunday evening.'

'I won't go to Juba's!'

'Yes, you will. You're a pain in the neck sometimes, but you're basically a good kid. You won't give me anything extra to worry about. Now, goodnight.'

She tried to kiss me, but I pulled away from her. She went back to the kitchen.

I turned my light on again. 'I'll show her,' I grumbled. I half hoped Tammy would hear me and come back so that we could have a fight, but if she heard me, she stayed away.

Picking up my world atlas, I plotted a course across Russia—a rough, difficult, dangerous trip that I would send Tammy on. One way.

Once Mom was soundly packed off to Siberia, I turned out the light and settled down into bed, feeling very pleased with myself.

Minutes later, I got down from my bunk, went into the kitchen and kissed Mom goodnight. She hugged me tightly and kissed me, too. Then I went back to bed.

It wouldn't be right to go to sleep without a goodnight kiss from Mom. I'm not even sure the sun would rise the next morning.

After that, I couldn't leave her in Siberia. I brought her back, so that she'd be here when I woke up.

TEN

DANGER IN THE DARK

Of course, I did go to Juba's after my job at the Trojan Horse. I tried complaining to her about Tammy, but she wouldn't let me.

Juba tried her best to make me feel better. She took me to Riverdale Farm, even though she says her legs aren't what they used to be. We played hours of cribbage, drank tea from her special china cups, and she let me stay up, watching television, far later than Tammy would have allowed me to. Juba made a bed for me on her living-room couch so I could watch TV in bed, 'just like a rich lady'.

It was fun, but I kept thinking of Mom and the boys. I had a hard time imagining what sort of place the group home was.

Mom had said it was like a boarding school, but the only boarding schools I knew about were in British school stories. I couldn't picture the boys in one of those places, although they would look cute in school uniforms.

Then I thought they were going to a work-house, like in *Oliver Twist*, but Mom wouldn't put them in a place like that.

I was eager for them to get back, but if I showed any interest in the place, Mom might think I was OK with her plan.

I wasn't OK with it.

Mom and the boys returned around eight o'clock Sunday night, just before Juba and I got back to our apartment.

The social worker with the slime dripping from her fangs was just leaving as we arrived.

'Hello, Khyber,' she said. She'd obviously been coached by Mom. 'How are you?'

I started to walk past her.

'Khyber,' Mom said in her warning voice.

'Fine, thank you,' I mumbled. I wasn't fine, but that was none of her business.

'I'll see you soon,' she said to Mom, then left. I took the boys into the living room. We played with their button collection.

'How did it go?' Mom asked Juba. She meant, 'Did my daughter behave herself?'

I didn't have to listen to the answer. Juba doesn't believe in double punishment. If I had acted like a jerk, Juba would have dealt with me herself, and been done with it.

When Mom kissed me goodnight, she didn't say anything about her weekend with the boys, and I didn't ask her.

The next day was Monday. My suspension was over. I went back to school.

I timed my walk so I'd arrive at school just before the bell rang. That way I wouldn't have to talk to anybody in the school yard.

Miss Melon practically licked her lips with delight when I walked into class. She kept me at the front with her during the singing of 'O, Canada'.

When that was over, the class sat down. Most were tittering and smirking. A few looked like they felt sorry for me. They were the ones who had their own difficulties with Tiffany.

Tiffany had been told I'd have to apologize, and she, of course, had spread that around.

'Tiffany, will you come up here, please,' Miss Melon said. 'Khyber has something she'd like to say to you.'

Tiffany's nose was so high in the air it almost scraped the paint off the ceiling.

'Keep it simple and keep it dignified,' Tammy

had told me. She had practised it with me, pretending to be Tiffany. 'Think of it as a character-building exercise.'

I've got enough character, I thought, as I straightened my back, but I said my apology just as I'd rehearsed it with Tammy.

Everyone seemed disappointed I didn't slug her again.

Miss Melon followed it up with a lecture on the importance of good citizenship, using me as an example of how not to behave. I knew nobody was listening to her, but it made me feel lousy just the same.

When I got home on Wednesday afternoon, Mom and the boys were out. Mom had told me at breakfast they had an appointment at Sick Kids, but I'd forgotten. I was already grumpy, and having them gone made me even grumpier.

'Come right home after school and stay here,' Tammy had told me. She didn't like me going out when she wasn't around.

The apartment felt empty and lonely. It was raining outside, off and on. There wasn't any sun to shine in through the windows, and the apartment was as dark and grey as the day outside.

I put one of Mom's Monkees records on, just for company.

Tammy had left out some potatoes for me to peel for supper, but I was too grumpy to do them.

I picked up my homework, then put it down again. I wandered around the apartment and into my brothers' room.

Mom had packed their clothes and toys into boxes.

I didn't stop to think about it. I went right to work, unpacked all the boxes, hung up their shirts, put their toys back on the shelves, folded sweaters and T-shirts into drawers. I gathered up all the empty boxes and carried them out to the balcony.

Looking down from the balcony, I saw X standing in the park, waiting for me. She hadn't been around all week. It was good to see her.

Halfway through making X a sandwich, I remembered that I wasn't supposed to leave the apartment. Could I be back before Mom returned? Yes, probably, and if not, Mom wouldn't mind me dashing out to give X something to eat. At least, I hoped she wouldn't.

By the time I got down to the street, X had

gone. It was getting even darker out. Putting the boys' things away must have taken more time than I'd thought. I could see X a block or so away on Gerrard, heading towards Allan Gardens, and I hurried after her.

If I'd known her real name, I could have yelled it out, and maybe she would have stopped. I could have handed her the sandwich and rushed back home before Tammy found that I'd left. The whole mess that followed could have been avoided.

But I didn't know X's real name, and even if I had, I couldn't have yelled it out. She would have thought it was the secret police calling her.

So, once I'd decided to take X the sandwich, there was no way to avoid The Trouble. Of course, if I hadn't taken the empty boxes out to the balcony, I wouldn't have seen X, and therefore would have been obediently at home when Mom got there. If Mom hadn't packed away my brothers' things, I wouldn't have had to unpack them, and wouldn't have been carrying the empty boxes on to the balcony, from where I saw X. So, in a way, the whole mess that happened was Tammy's fault.

How's that for passing the buck?

I caught up with X at Allan Gardens. She

was on a bench inside the park a little way. I sat down at the other end of the bench and passed her the sandwich.

'I can't stay very long,' I said. 'In fact, I have to get back home right away.'

X pushed her blue suitcase a bit under the bench with her feet. She didn't reach for the sandwich. I pushed it towards her a bit more.

'Here—here's a sandwich. I've got to go!' I stood up. X still hadn't moved. I started to walk away, then turned back and looked at her. She was hunched down into her trench coat. She looked very sad and very lonely.

I sat back down. What else could I do? She probably wouldn't have eaten if I'd gone away, and who knew when she'd eaten last? Maybe not since the last time we'd seen each other.

Tammy would understand. If she didn't, I'd be doing chores and extra arithmetic again, but I'd deal with that when the time came.

I took some deep breaths to calm down, to help X feel comfortable, the way I do with the boys sometimes. I'm never in a hurry when I see her. She probably thought at first that I was someone from the secret police, just pretending to be Khyber.

I relaxed, then she relaxed, and once I started talking, she started eating.

'Mom's got this idea in her head to send my brothers away. How can she do that? Parents don't send their kids away!'

I changed the subject then, and rattled on about the best places to find snakes in India, which I'd been reading about lately. By the time I ran out of things to say about snakes, X had almost finished her sandwich.

'Have you ever heard the soup song?' X didn't answer, of course, so I started singing it. As I was taking a deep breath before the final line, X spoke, so softly that I didn't hear her at first.

'I used to be a folk singer.'

The deep breath I'd taken drained quietly out of my body.

'I used to sing folk songs in Yorkville.' Yorkville is the part of Toronto where the hippies used to hang out in the sixties. I tried to imagine X as a hippie, with love beads around her neck and a guitar over her shoulder. I couldn't picture it.

'Is that when the secret police started following you?'

X didn't answer me. As I waited for her to

say something more, I realized how late it had got. The afternoon had gone. Night time had come. By now, Mom and the boys would be back. I wished I'd left a note.

X started singing. Her voice was raspy and tuneless, as though her brain could remember singing, but the memory hadn't got down as far as her voice yet.

'Where have all the flowers gone?' she sang. I knew the song. I sang it with her. We sat on that park bench in the growing darkness, with bits of rain dripping down on us, and we softly sang to the park. We went from one song to another. I forgot the rest of the world existed.

'Hey, what is this? A bloody Girl Guide meeting?'

The rude voice jolted me back to reality.

A pack of skinheads had crept up behind us, and we were now surrounded.

Tammy hadn't needed to warn me to stay away from skinheads. Everything about these folk smelled of trouble. (In fact, everything about them smelled.) They wore heavy black boots and military coats with Nazi symbols and skulls on them. They had shaved heads. They didn't even have hair to cover up part of their ugly faces.

At one time, they must have all been little pink babies, cute and gurgly, but that was as hard for me to imagine as X being a hippie.

'Never judge people as a group,' Tammy was always saying to me. 'Judge them as individuals.' But it's hard to judge people as individuals when they travel in packs and all act the same.

'X, let's get going,' I said quietly, slowly standing up. These people are wild animals, I thought. I'll keep calm, and move slowly, and they won't attack.

X had disappeared into her trench coat, like a turtle into its shell. She wasn't moving.

'They shouldn't allow trash like this in the park,' one of them said, kicking at X's leg.

'X, come on, let's go,' I pleaded, but X acted as if she didn't hear me.

'X? What kind of a name is that? X? Short for Extra-defective?' The guy who said that was fat, bald, and ugly. He looked like he swallowed beer cans whole. He thought he had made a joke, and he laughed. The other skinheads laughed with him.

'What's in the bag, Defect?' One of them grabbed for X's suitcase. X was frozen.

'Leave her alone!' I yelled, giving him a push.

He laughed and pushed me back. I fell into the mud. I bounced up again and rushed at him, but the big one got in my way.

'What are you so excited about?'

I punched him hard in his blubbery stomach. He doubled over, clutching himself. I jumped around him and saw the others punching and pulling at X. One of them had her suitcase.

Maybe they weren't real skinheads at all. Maybe they were with the secret police.

I leapt at them with a shriek that David and Daniel would have been proud to make. I don't know which one I landed on. I wasn't aiming for any jerk in particular.

At that point, I lost track of what was happening. I know I was being kicked, punched, and shoved, and I also know that I got in a few good kicks and punches of my own.

The fight was broken up by a police siren. The cops hadn't come for us—they kept driving right on by the park—but it was enough to send the skinheads back into the cover of the trees.

X and I were sprawled out on the ground. I crawled over to her. 'X, are you OK?' I put my head down close to hers. She was moaning a bit. 'Can you get up?'

Rain was starting to come down for real. I shook X again. 'Let me help you up.'

Her suitcase had been yanked open. There was nothing inside. I scrambled around on the ground, looking for any jewels or secret papers the skinheads might have dropped when they made their getaway. I couldn't find anything.

Leaning against the bench, X struggled to her feet. I closed the suitcase and handed it to her. She looked all hunched in and ashamed.

'You should see a doctor. Do you want me to go with you to the hospital?'

X turned away from me, as if she didn't want me to see her. I asked her again, but she just shrugged down into herself and walked away.

I headed home, wondering what to tell Tammy. She'd forbidden me to fight, so I couldn't tell her the truth. The best lie I could come up with was that I'd slipped and fallen, and that's how I got my clothes dirty. It was a pretty lame lie. Not even I believed it.

The skinheads were still in the park, right at the corner I'd have to pass. I was sure they were waiting for me.

Forgetting all the rules of Elmer the Safety Elephant—who never had to deal with skinheads—

I dashed into the street, narrowly avoiding several cars that honked angrily. I headed south, then east, through the school yard, and up into Regent Park. I entered my building the back way.

Mom was home. She was furious. First she hugged me, because she was glad I was safe. Then she glared at me with a face of stone and ice.

'Well?'

I told her as much truth as I could, without getting myself into more trouble. 'I'm sorry about the potatoes, Mom. I was just about to do them when I saw X outside waiting for me, so I took her a sandwich, and tried to leave right away, but then she started talking and . . . singing. We sang together for a bit, then she went her way, and I headed home, only I slipped and fell in the mud. That's why I'm all dirty.' I stopped for a breath, and to see how well my lie was going over. Tammy's expression hadn't changed. I could tell she knew I was lying.

'Go and get washed for supper. Put your pyjamas on. You're going right to bed after you do the dishes.'

I was very muddy, so I jumped in the shower. Parts of my body were very sore. I felt myself all over to see if anything was broken. Everything seemed in one piece. There was blood in several places where their hard boots had kicked me. The hot water felt good. I wanted to cry, but I didn't.

Supper was on the table when I got out. We were having soup poured over mashed potatoes. I wanted to tell Tammy about singing X the soup song, but her face was still angry, so I didn't say anything.

When the dishes were done, I went to bed. I tried to do my homework there for a while, until Tammy turned off my light. 'You had your chance to do that earlier,' she said. She did kiss me good-night, but it didn't feel like she meant it.

ELEVEN

MUD

When I got to school the next morning, the windows were boarded up. Not all the windows. Just the ones in Miss Melon's classroom.

'What happened?' I asked a kid in my home-room class.

'Somebody broke all the windows in Melon-ball's class last night. Threw mud and leaves and stuff all over the classroom, too.'

'How do you know?'

'Overheard the teachers.'

'Do they know who did it?'

'Probably somebody who didn't like Miss Melon.'

There was a strange feeling in the class all that morning. The boards on the windows made the classroom dark and eerie, even though all the lights were on.

The other kids were acting strange, too.

They'd look at me, and look away again.

I stood alone at the fence during morning recess. Some kid was throwing a ball against the boards where the windows used to be, until a teacher yelled at him to knock it off.

Tiffany and her gang walked by. They looked at me and laughed. I turned my back to them so I wouldn't have to see their goofy faces.

Mom was coming up the sidewalk towards the school. I raised my hand to wave at her. Just then, she looked at me, and I stopped my hand in midwave. She looked angry, disappointed, and . . . hopeless.

I didn't have to wait long to find out what was going on. As soon as we got back to class after recess, Miss Melon gave the class some chapters to read. Then she looked at me and said, 'Come with me.'

She held my arm all the way to the principal's office.

The same gang of sour adults was there, minus Tiffany's mother. A cop was with them. He was ten feet tall.

I was getting scared. This wasn't like my last visit to the principal's office, where I knew I'd be punished, but I didn't care. I knew then that what I had done was right, even if it was wrong, if you know what I mean.

This time, I didn't even know what I had done, although I was pretty sure they all thought I had done something.

And this time, Tammy wasn't jumping up and down to defend me. She just sat still. She also looked very, very tired.

The principal was the only one who spoke. He called me by my unmentionable name. I listened for Tammy to correct him, but she said nothing.

'As you know, there was damage done to the school last night. We're trying to get to the bottom of it, and we'd like to know where you were yesterday evening.'

'I was at home.'

'Before you were at home.'

'I was in Allan Gardens with . . .' I started to say 'with X', but I didn't want the cop to know about her. 'With a friend,' I said instead.

'What is the name and address of this friend?'

I looked at the cop. He towered above everyone, and his frown was aimed at me.

'Answer the question.'

'Am I in trouble?' I asked, my voice sounding very small.

'You were seen running away from the school last night. You returned home with your clothes torn and muddy, and you could not give your mother an explanation of how they got that way. Yes, I'd say you were in trouble.'

I stared at Tammy, my jaw dropping to my chest. My mother had ratted on me to the enemy. She had never done that before. I had believed, deep down inside me, that she never would.

Tammy looked right back at me, but there was nothing in her face or eyes to make me feel better.

I looked away from her.

'I didn't break those windows.'

'Then where were you last night?'

'I told you. I was in Allan Gardens with a friend.'

'If you were in Allan Gardens, why were you running away from the school?'

I had no answer for that.

'Will you at least tell us the name of the friend you were with?'

I looked at Tammy again. She knew I was with X! Why didn't she say so? But she said nothing. She just sat in the chair and looked at her hands.

I stopped being afraid then and started getting angry.

'I will not give you her name,' I said, loudly and clearly, looking the principal straight in his little pig eyes. He looked like someone from the secret police. No wonder X was afraid of them.

'There is no friend,' Tammy finally spoke up, but what she said horrified me.

'Khyber has an imaginary friend she calls X, but there really isn't such a person. She makes sandwiches for herself to eat in the park after school, but she tells me they're for her friend X so I won't think she's eating more than her share. We're on a tight budget,' she explained.

Tammy's words made me cold and numb all over.

The principal spoke. 'In that case, (unmentionable name), you leave us no choice. You're a bright girl, and we've bent over backwards to give you every advantage, but you're choosing instead to waste your talents. You are unable or unwilling to clear your name. I'm sorry to have to put the burden of your misbehaviour back on your mother, but you have forced us to do this.'

He stood up, as if he were about to issue a royal decree.

'This school no longer has a place for you. Consider yourself expelled.'

Expelled! 'You can't expel me,' I shouted, 'because I quit!'

I turned and left the room. I tried to slam the door, but it had one of those slow-closing things on it. It's impossible to slam doors like that.

I moved through the office so fast, I knocked piles of papers off the desk and slammed into a teacher who was unscrewing the lid of a jar of green paint. The paint splattered all over the teacher's sweater. Unfortunately, I was too angry to enjoy it.

My anger gave me power. My rage made me giddy. I was glad they had expelled me! I'd never have to go back there again!

I got my stuff out of my locker—all that I wanted of it, anyway—crammed the padlock into my back pocket and gave the locker door a good, hard slam. You can slam locker doors, and I slammed mine two or three more times—not out of temper, but just because I felt like it.

A teacher stuck her head out of the classroom door and said something stern, but I didn't care. I laughed and laughed my way out of the school.

Then Tammy caught up with me, and I stopped laughing.

'I can't believe you're acting like this,' she said. 'Now, on top of everything else that I have to deal with, I've got to find another school for you. Plus, I have to pay for the windows you broke. How am I going to do that?'

I stopped walking. 'Mom, you know I didn't break those windows!'

'I don't know that, Khyber. You lied to me about where you were and what you were doing last night, telling me you were with some imaginary friend, which you really should have outgrown a long time ago. You come home covered in mud, and you disobeyed me by being out in the first place. No, I certainly do not know that you didn't break those windows.'

It felt like I was walking with a stranger, with someone who didn't know me.

It was a very lonely, very sad feeling.

The gutters along the edge of the sidewalk were filled with muddy rainwater. Bits of garbage floated by.

'You are unable or unwilling to clear your name,' the principal had said.

A clear name. I pictured a cold mountain

stream, running fast, but clear enough to see straight through to the pebbles at the bottom.

My name is like the water in the gutter, I thought. I have to get it like the mountain stream. I have to clear my name.

Until I did, my name was Mud.

TWELVE

TAKING LEAVE

Mom and I didn't speak to each other for the rest of the day.

I stayed out of her way, on my bunk, but I didn't feel like reading and I didn't feel like looking at my atlases.

After supper, Juba came over. She and Mom talked in the kitchen while I got the twins ready for bed. Their stuff was off the shelves and out of their drawers again, but the boxes weren't around. Tammy must have stashed them in her room. I did not go in there to check.

I couldn't think of anything to say to Mom that would make things better.

When my brothers were in their pyjamas, I went to bed. I hurt in a lot of places, and I had big, purple bruises all over my body.

I felt lost and alone, and I cried until I fell asleep.

Tammy didn't come to my alcove to kiss me goodnight.

I woke up a few hours later.

The apartment was quiet. I looked out of the window at the life on the street, and wondered what was going to happen the next day.

Tammy would probably make me stick with her all the time, in case I got a sudden urge to rush off and break some more windows. She'd still be mad at me, of course. She'd still think I broke the school windows. She'd still think she couldn't trust me.

She might not talk to me all day. She might be so angry and disappointed, she wouldn't have anything to say to me.

I felt completely and utterly alone.

I could go into her room, wake her up, and confess that I had been fighting. She'd punish me for fighting, but I could handle punishment.

I was halfway down my ladder when I remembered that Mom didn't believe that X was a real person. If she didn't believe that, she wouldn't believe that I was fighting skinheads to defend her.

If only I could provide her with proof, but what proof did I have? I couldn't very well go up to the skinheads and say, 'Excuse me, you ugly creatures, would you mind very much telling my mother that you were beating me up last night when I was supposed to be breaking windows?'

Sure.

I crawled back into bed.

X was my only hope. If I could tell X what had happened, she might agree to speak to my mom. At least then I could prove to Mom that X wasn't some 'imaginary friend'.

But X might not be back in the neighbourhood for days—longer, maybe, since she was probably afraid she'd get beaten up again.

I sat up on my elbows. There was only one way out of this. I'd have to go out and find X, and bring her back here. She'd be nervous, at first, at meeting Mom, but I thought she'd trust me enough to believe me when I told her that Mom was not a member of the secret police.

Tammy would never let me go off on my own, and once I started another school, I'd be trapped. My only choice was to go tonight. With a bit of luck, I'd bring X home in time for breakfast.

I waited a while longer, to make sure Tammy was sound asleep so she wouldn't hear me. I planned everything out in my head, so that I'd know just what to do when I got down from my bunk.

When I had it all planned out, I crept down, got dressed and went into the kitchen. I made a couple of peanut butter and corn syrup sandwiches, cringing with every sound. Food might help persuade X to come back with me.

I left Mom a note on the kitchen table. It read, 'Gone to find X.' I signed it, 'Love, Khyber.'

I put my key around my neck, tucked it under my sweater and grabbed my jacket.

Out on the street, I took a last look at our building. David was standing at his bedroom window, looking out. He was flapping his arms. It looked like he was waving goodbye.

THIRTEEN

TIRED FEET

It was a pretty dumb idea.

If all the secret police couldn't find X, with all of their spy tools like telephones in their shoes and jet-propelled umbrellas, how was I going to find her? All I had were two peanut butter and corn syrup sandwiches, and neither of them contained a secret camera or even a scrap of microfilm.

It was a dumb idea to continue.

It would have been even dumber to go home without at least trying to find her.

I started walking.

I had walked past the library when I remembered the pouch full of wedding money under my mattress. If I had been smart, I would have brought that with me. I wasn't smart.

The night world is a different place from the day world. It's got the same buildings and streets and everything, but everything looks different, everything sounds different, everything feels different.

The last time I was outside at this time of night was when Tammy and I took the boys to the hospital. I thought I was miserable that night. I wasn't. Compared to how I felt now, I was happy that night.

I think people feel more invisible at night. During the day, it's light out, and everyone can see you. During the night, you're just a shadow. You become part of the darkness.

I felt like a shadow, too, until a police car drove by, and then I felt very visible. I turned out of the light of the street lamps and into the darkness of Allan Gardens.

There were lights around the main path, but the rest of the park was in shadows. The wind was blowing the dead leaves around on the ground, and the tree branches squeaked when they rubbed together. Something horrible could be behind every tree.

In the darkness, I stumbled over something and fell smack on my face into the grass. The something I'd tripped over moaned.

I jumped up as if I'd been hit by an electric bolt, and turned to look at what I'd tripped over.

A man was sleeping on the ground. No blanket, no sleeping bag, no anything. He must have been cold.

He rolled over on to his back, and his arm flopped out towards me. I thought he was reaching for me, and I took off like a shot.

Allan Gardens, the park I'd been to a thousand times, the park I'd taken my brothers to and sat with X in was now a place of horror. 'How about the Haunted Allan Gardens?' I said out loud, as if I was talking to Tammy. 'Ghosts could jump out at you from behind trees, and park benches could come alive.'

The headlights of the cars going past the park made the shadows move. Everything looked like it was going to grab me.

I was scared silly being there, but I kept at it. Soon there was just one section left to check—the area behind the greenhouse. So far, none of the people I'd seen sleeping on park benches was X.

Close to the end of the park, I was looking the wrong way when a man stepped out of the shadows. He must have been looking the wrong way, too. We bumped into each other and both let out a yell. I ran. I didn't look to see what he did.

I kept running, not stopping until I was almost at Yonge Street. I didn't feel like a brave explorer. I felt like just what I was—a scared kid in a huge city at night, looking for a woman who didn't want to be found.

I headed north on Yonge.

Yonge Street is Toronto's main street. It's the longest street in the country, or in the world, or maybe even in the universe. It stretches from Lake Ontario to very, very far in the north, maybe all the way to the North Pole.

I hoped I wouldn't have to go that far.

I needed to think. I sat on the steps of a dress shop, scrunching back against a doorway so I wouldn't be seen. There weren't a lot of people out on the street, but there were some. I wanted to be invisible.

X needed to be invisible, too. She would stay in the shadows. She wouldn't go where there were big windows and bright lights. She wouldn't go into doughnut shops.

She would stick to dark places—parks, alleys, back streets. There had to be a million places like that in Toronto. How could I search them all?

The answer was, I couldn't, and even if I

could, X was not going to sit still and wait for me to get to her. I could search one alley, and leave it just as she was slipping into it from the other end.

I'd just have to do the best I could, and maybe I'd get lucky.

There was an alley that ran behind Yonge Street. I started walking there, but it was too scary. All those corners and narrow doorways—they were completely dark. I didn't have a flashlight so the only way to check them would be to step into the darkness and feel around. I couldn't bring myself to do that. If X was there, and she felt someone grab her in the dark, she'd think it was the secret police, and she'd run away. If X wasn't there, well, I didn't want to know what was.

I decided to stick to the main street. I'd search those alley places during the day.

I kept heading north. Almost every doorway had somebody sleeping in it. Some of the sleepers were just sprawled out on the cement. Others had blankets. Some had big pieces of cardboard underneath them, to keep out the chill of the pavement.

I wondered where all these people went when the stores opened up.

By the time the sky got light, and the streets began to be busy with people heading to work, I had got as far as Eglinton Avenue, which is a long, long way from Regent Park.

There were skyscrapers here, and shops that were fancier than any place Tammy had ever shopped in.

I could smell bacon cooking in some of the restaurants.

I was exhausted, and I had to go to the toilet. I went into a doughnut shop.

'Washrooms are for customers only,' the woman behind the counter said, glaring at me. She was rude, like Valerie, but I didn't feel anything good behind the rudeness—just more rudeness.

She was very busy with customers. When she turned to fetch someone a blueberry muffin, I snatched the washroom key from the little peg on the wall. I'd be done before she knew it was missing.

The face in the washroom mirror didn't look much like mine. Its eyes were puffy, and it looked scared. I splashed cold water on it. That didn't help. Now my face looked puffy, scared, and wet.

There were no paper towels, so I dried my

face on my sweater and left the washroom. I heard the door click behind me as I realized I'd left the key in there. I left the doughnut shop in a hurry. For all I knew, locking the key in the washroom was a crime.

This didn't seem to be the sort of neighbourhood where X would feel comfortable. There weren't as many poor people out on the streets. X would stick out too much here. I crossed the street and headed back downtown.

I kept walking until I reached Mount Pleasant Cemetery. It looked so warm and quiet that I decided to go there, just for a moment, to sit down.

Tammy and the boys and I often walked in the graveyard near our place, next to Riverdale Farm. It was a very old graveyard, with winding paths and lots of trees and squirrels.

This graveyard was different—more open— but still very beautiful.

I found a private spot in the sunshine, near some graves but not on top of any, in case the people buried there wouldn't like it. I sat down.

By now, Tammy and the boys would be awake. She'd have found my note on the kitchen table. I could see them all there, in the kitchen, eating breakfast. I wished I were there with them.

I stretched out on the grass. The sun was warm, and I was tired. It wasn't long before I fell asleep.

FOURTEEN

WIN SOME, LOSE SOME

When I woke up, it was early afternoon. The crushing sleepy feeling was gone from my head, but the rest of me sure felt lousy. I was sore from the skinhead beating and stiff from lying on the ground. The sun had disappeared behind some clouds, and I was shivering.

I was also hungry, and I needed to go to the toilet.

After making sure no one was around, I ducked into some bushes and went. How does X manage, I wondered? Does she use the bushes, too?

I started walking down Yonge Street again. Walking warmed me up a little, and once I got moving I didn't feel so stiff. It was an easier walk this time—mostly downhill.

'Spare some change?'

I looked round. 'Are you talking to me?' I asked the two people wrapped in a blanket, sitting in a doorway.

'You and everybody else,' the woman grinned. 'You don't happen to have any spare change, do you?'

I shook my head. 'Not a cent. Oh, you have a little dog!'

'His name's Winsome,' the man said. 'You know, you win some, you lose some?'

Winsome licked my face as I petted him. The woman made room for me on her blanket, and I sat down with them.

'My name's Carolyn, and this is Hammond.' We shook hands.

Hammond had long hair pulled back in a ponytail, and rings in several places on his face. Carolyn had shorter hair, all curly.

'My name's Khyber.'

'Winsome's hungry,' Carolyn said. 'We're trying to get money to buy him some food.'

'I have some food,' I said, digging out one of my sandwiches. That still left me with one for X. 'It's peanut butter and corn syrup. Is that OK for dogs?'

'At this point, he'll eat anything, but we don't want to take your lunch.'

I told them not to worry about that. Carolyn took the sandwich and divided it into three pieces. I don't know who ate the fastest.

'You're hungry, too,' I said.

'We just got into town yesterday,' Hammond said. 'We hitchhiked here from Sault Sainte Marie.'

I pictured the map of Ontario in my mind. 'That's in the corner of Lake Superior.'

'Smart kid.'

'I'm going to go there someday,' I said. 'I'm going to go everywhere. I'm going to be an explorer.'

'I'm going to be a vet,' Carolyn said. 'I like animals better than people—well, better than most people. Hammond is a poet. He'll write poems about the animals I cure.'

'I know lots of animal poems,' I said. 'Would you like to hear one?'

'Sure.'

I told them 'The Owl and the Pussycat'. It's loaded with animals. While I was saying it, a small crowd gathered. When I got to the end, where they dance by the light of the moon, everyone applauded a bit. Some dropped money in the little box in front of Carolyn.

Wait till I tell Tammy, I thought, and then I remembered what I was supposed to be doing.

'I'm looking for someone.' I described X. They hadn't seen her.

I sat with them a while longer. While I patted Winsome, they told me all about their trip from Sault Sainte Marie to Toronto, and I told them all about the Khyber Pass. I thought about singing them the soup song, but it made me homesick just to think about it. We talked and we watched people's legs go by.

'I know where you can get a job,' I said. 'You'll get a meal out of it, anyway, if she likes you.' I told them about the Trojan Horse. 'Ask for Valerie. She'll be very rude to you, but don't worry about that. Tell her I sent you,' I added.

I got up and said goodbye.

'You're in some kind of trouble, aren't you, Khyber?'

I nodded.

'The streets aren't safe for you,' Hammond said. 'They aren't safe for us, and we're adults. You'd be most welcome to hang out with us for as long as you'd like.'

'Thanks, but I have to find my friend.'

I gave Winsome a final pat, and started walking again.

FIFTEEN

BENCH-SITTING

When I finally sat down on a bench at the Eaton Centre shopping mall, I thought I would never be able to move again. I'd gone on long walks before with Tammy and the twins, but I'd always known where I was going, how far away it was, and when I'd be home again. This time I didn't know if I was nearing the end of my journey or I was just beginning.

I was hungry, too, and I kept thinking of that sandwich in my bag. Food was everywhere. People walked by me with ice cream cones, and I could smell hamburgers frying and popcorn popping. There were egg rolls, cabbage rolls, cinnamon rolls and rolls stuffed with ham and cheese.

There was food all around me, but I couldn't have any of it. I wished, again, that I had brought my wedding money with me.

The mall was warm. I kept nodding off and

waking up again with a jolt. I saw a security guard looking at me, so I hauled myself to my feet and staggered away.

I knew I should have been out on the street looking for X, but I was so tired, I stayed in the mall. I guess I was hoping that X would just walk by me, and then my search would be over.

I went from bench to bench, moving around every so often so no one would get suspicious.

This must be how X feels, I thought, always being watched, always being hunted. It was even worse for her. Security guards wear uniforms. You can spot them coming towards you in time to get out of their way. The secret police who were after X could be anybody.

I plunked myself down on a bench near the Queen Street exit. A woman on the other end of the bench was writing furiously in a note-book. I leaned over to see what she was writing.

'Hey!' she said, putting an arm over her work. 'Are you trying to steal my idea?'

'No. I'm looking for someone.'

'Aren't we all?'

'Are you looking for someone, too? Who are you looking for?'

'Someone who will buy my script.'

'You're writing a play? I was just in a play. I played an equilateral triangle. Would you like to hear my line?'

'No.'

'It was a pretty dumb play. What's yours about?'

'It's a movie script. It's about a woman who's an artistic genius, but she spends all of her time hanging out in a mall so no one will know she's a genius.'

'Why doesn't she want anyone to know?'

'It's part of her genius.'

I didn't know what to say to that, so I asked her if she'd seen X. She stopped talking about her stupid movie long enough to say she hadn't, then went right back to her script.

She was still talking about it when I left her and went back to the street.

It was getting close to supper time. The sky was beginning to look like an evening sky.

The sidewalks were crowded. I walked down to Front Street and over to the train station. I'd be able to sit down there. Maybe X had the same idea. No one would pay any attention to a woman with a blue suitcase in a train station.

The Toronto train station is probably the best place in the city. There are huge stone pillars out front that you have to walk through to get inside. Even before you've gone anywhere, you feel like you've gone somewhere.

I go there as often as I can persuade Tammy to take me. You can go up to any ticket window and ask how much it is to go somewhere, and they'll tell you. They'll even tell you how long it takes to get there, and what cities you'll pass through. I've never been on a train, and you can't go up to the platform without a ticket, but when I finally do get to ride on one, I know just how it will feel.

The train station was packed with people rushing to catch their trains. Nobody looked happy, even though it was the end of the working week, and they were heading home.

I looked around for X, but I didn't see her. After using the washroom, I went back outside.

I was tired and hungry. Yonge Street was so crowded that unless X passed right beside me, I'd never find her. It would help if I was taller. I could look over people's heads, rather than at their chests.

A rooftop! That was it! If I could get up on a rooftop, I could check out a whole block at one time. It was worth a try.

In the alley behind Yonge Street, I spotted ladders attached to the backs of some buildings. They looked awfully high up when I looked at them from the bottom. I picked one and started climbing.

On the roof, I felt a million feet tall. The city was below me, all lit up. Leaning against the wall at the edge of the roof, I looked down at people who had no idea I was looking at them.

Across the street, outside the Eaton Centre, someone was playing the drums. Someone else was doing a magic show, and someone else was talking about hell through a loud speaker. It was a wonderful sight!

There were lots of people below me, but no X. If I hadn't been hungry, tired, worried, and scared, I could have stayed up there for hours, watching what happened on the street.

But I was hungry, tired, worried, and scared, and being those things tends to take the fun out of whatever else you're doing.

After a little while, I climbed back down.

SIXTEEN

BLUE SUEDE SHOES

I was pretty dizzy when I got to the bottom of the ladder. Not eating and not sleeping can make you dizzy.

I plunked myself down on the pavement between two bins. The smell was horrible, but I was too tired to move again until I heard something rattle around in one of them.

Then I moved.

Night was falling. The streets were getting dark again.

I didn't want to be noticed, of course, but I also hated it that nobody noticed me. Didn't anybody care that an eleven-year-old girl was wandering around the city at night, all by herself?

People rushed past, busy with their own thoughts and plans and paying absolutely no attention to me.

I wandered into the army surplus store, but

I left right away. It hurt too much to be there without my brothers.

I kept walking.

Tired of Yonge Street, I turned east and headed over to Church Street. It was quieter, and X probably would prefer a quieter street.

By this point, my brain was thick with exhaustion and hunger. Suddenly, without even thinking about it, I sat down on the step of a boarded-up shop, took out X's sandwich, and started eating.

'I'll only eat half of it,' I decided, but by the time I decided that, the whole sandwich was gone.

Now what? With no food, X would never come back with me. Without a peanut butter and corn syrup sandwich to pass across a bench to her, X might not even recognize me.

I had caused Tammy worry and made her even more angry, and for what? For nothing.

My face hurt from trying not to cry.

Should I go home empty-handed, and hope Tammy would forgive me?

Should I just keep travelling? Maybe I could stow away on a steamship, or hide out on a freight train.

In time, Tammy would forget about me. She could even have another daughter, one who liked pink and trying on dresses.

I started walking again.

I couldn't see clearly because my eyes kept tearing up. I stumbled along the street, paying no attention to who I passed, or who passed me. If X was close by, I didn't notice.

Somebody bumped into me. I wiped my eyes and screamed.

I was staring at a monster! He had blood all over him and an eyeball slipping down one cheek.

'Please excuse me,' the monster said. 'It's a little hard to see through this mask.' He walked on.

Of course—it was Hallowe'en! I suddenly noticed that Church Street was filling up with strange creatures—gorillas, clowns, more monsters, men dressed as butterflies, and women with moustaches.

Tammy and I loved Hallowe'en. Mom adored dressing up, and Hallowe'en was the one night of the year she could do it without embarrassing me. We'd dress the twins up, too, and we'd go to the Hallowe'en party at the Regent Park community centre. We'd take Juba with us, although she wouldn't dress up. When we got back home, Tammy would make popcorn, and we'd stay up late. Sometimes Tammy would read aloud from Edgar Allen Poe. Sometimes we'd make up ghost stories of our own.

I sat down on a low wall around a parking lot, watching all the people go by in costume. They all looked like they were having a great time.

Tammy and the boys were probably at the community centre having a wonderful time at the Hallowe'en party. I wondered if they even missed me. I started to cry. I couldn't help it.

Once I started, I couldn't stop. I cried and I cried.

Then a van pulled up beside me, and Elvis stepped out.

SEVENTEEN

RETURN

Another Elvis followed the first one, and another after that. I counted them as they piled out. There were a dozen Elvises standing around in the parking lot.

'Hey, look! It's our fan club!' one Elvis said, pointing at me. I was even more surprised. Elvis was a woman! They were all women!

'I suppose she wants an autograph,' another Elvis said. 'Oh, the price of fame!'

They laughed and joked like that for a minute. Then one of them said, 'Hey, she's crying! What's wrong, honey?'

I wiped my face quickly, but it was too late. The Elvises gathered around me. One of them put her arm round my shoulders. It felt so much like Tammy's arm that I started to cry again.

'It's OK. You can tell us what's wrong.'
'Maybe we can help.'

I tried talking, but the sobs choked off my voice.

'She can't talk until she stops crying.'

'Let's do one of our numbers for her. That will cheer her up.'

'Or make her cry harder.'

'Would you like to hear one of our numbers?' Elvis asked me.

I nodded.

'She said yes! Places, everybody! I'll introduce us.'

Everyone took their places. 'Ladies and gentlemen,' she began. I looked around. There was no one watching but me.

'We proudly present—The All Girls Elvis Group!'

'TAGEG for short.'

'A one and a two and . . .' They started belting out 'Jailhouse Rock'.

The All Girls Elvis Group was really terrible, but they did stop me from crying. They sounded even worse than I do when I sing the soup song.

They took their bows as I applauded.

'Now, my dear. Tell us what's wrong.'

I told them the story. What else could I do? When a bunch of women make fools out of themselves to help you feel better, you kind of have to trust them.

I told them everything, about Mom and my brothers, the fight with the skinheads, the broken windows, and my need to find X. I talked until I ran out of words.

'Come with us,' Elvis said. 'Let's go call your mother. Then we'll drive you home. We've got plenty of time before our performance.'

'Yeah, and no one's all that anxious to hear us, anyway.'

I could believe that. 'But I can't go home!' I protested.

'Yes, you can,' Elvis insisted, and at that moment, I knew she was right. I could.

'There's a pay phone right across the street.' Elvis pointed. 'As soon as Dracula finishes his phone call, we'll call your mom.'

'We don't have a phone,' I told them. 'It was disconnected.'

'That sounds familiar,' one of them said. 'Well, we'll just drive on over there, then.'

'I live in Regent Park,' I said, in case she didn't want to drive there.

'Perfect,' she said. 'So does Elvis over there.'

'Yup, Elvis is alive and well and living in

Regent Park,' said the Regent Park Elvis.

The Regent Park Elvis gave me her address and phone number, and I told her where our apartment was. All the Elvises gave me a hug. Then the driving Elvis and I climbed into the van and headed for home.

Elvis came up to the apartment with me. Mom was waiting at the open door. I felt her arms go around me, and I knew everything would be all right.

Mom was so glad to see me she almost forgot to thank Elvis for bringing me home, and that's very glad, because Mom's big on thank-yous!

The boys were still awake. We all went into the living room, and Mom and I hugged and cried, and the boys played with their button collection, and that was the end of the adventure.

EIGHTEEN

ROUND-UP

Nothing ever really ends, though. Things go on and on. They change shape sometimes, but they still go on and on. After we got through crying, Mom and I talked until we fell asleep next to David and Daniel, right in the living room. We started talking again as soon as we woke up the next morning.

Tammy apologized to me for not believing me about the windows. They found the kids who did it. They didn't even go to that school. They didn't know they were breaking Miss Melon's windows. They didn't know Miss Melon.

She also said she knew me well enough to know that I wouldn't leave in the middle of the night to find somebody named X unless there really was somebody named X. She said she was sorry she hadn't believed me.

The principal phoned Tammy and said they'd be glad to take me back. Tammy told him to go suck an egg, or words to that effect.

I told Tammy about the fight with the skin-heads, and she wanted to go right out with her rolling pin to teach them a lesson, but I convinced her not to. The whole thing already seemed like a long time ago.

I was with Mom the day the social worker drove us and the boys to the group home. They were going to live there.

The social worker wasn't as bad as I thought. Her fangs weren't nearly as long, and she wasn't as slimy as she was when I first met her. She treated the boys well, and they seemed to like her, and that's the important thing.

The group home was really nice. It was a big house on a small farm out in the countryside, near a small town. It was quiet, with hardly any cars around. It was also right next door to a provincial park, so they could go for long walks. The staff liked special kids like Daniel and David, and they planned to teach them to do things.

Coming back to the apartment the night after the boys moved out was awful. Juba came over, and I called the Regent Park Elvis and she came over (although she didn't look like Elvis any more). That got us through the first night, but there were a lot more to come that were just as hard.

Tammy enrolled me in a new school, but I didn't like it any better than the last one, and they didn't like me. Tammy didn't know what to do with herself during the day. For five years, David and Daniel took up all her time, and now they were gone.

We tried to pretend we were cheerful, but we weren't fooling each other. If we could have seen the boys regularly, it would have been different, but there was no bus service from Toronto to the group home, and the social worker was too busy to drive us there.

Everything I used to love fell flat—Saturday morning breakfast, working the weddings, going to the library, even looking at my atlases—everything. Even the soup song didn't sound right without David and Daniel around to hear it.

One night at supper, Mom put down her fork and said, 'I can't do this any more, Khyber. I can't stand not being able to be with the boys.'

'You mean we can bring them back here to live with us?'

Tammy shook her head. 'No, we can't do that. I still think they're in the best place for them right now.' She started to smile. 'How would you like it if we went to live near them?'

It didn't take me long to decide I would like it very much.

Once again, the Elvises came to our rescue. The driving Elvis drove us to the small town. We found a house with an apartment for rent over the garage. It's one mile from the group home and one mile from the town. The Elvises are helping us move in a couple of days.

Mom's talking about going back to school.

When I went to work last Saturday, I told Valerie we were moving. Carolyn and Hammond are working there now, part-time, in exchange for a bed in the basement and three meals a day. Valerie complains about the dog, but I saw her feeding him when she thought no one was looking.

'Your mom already told me you were leaving,' Valerie said. 'Here, take this. It's a goodbye present.'

I started to cry. Valerie had bought me the greatest backpack in the world.

Valerie tried to be rude when I said goodbye, but instead she started to cry, too, and gave me a great big hug in front of everyone in the restaurant! She'll probably never live that down.

Juba cried, too, when we told her we were leaving. We all cried, and for a little while, I wished we weren't going.

'I wish Juba could come with us,' I said to Tammy. 'I wish Valerie could come, too. She could work in the restaurant in town. She would have a whole new crowd of people to be rude to.'

'For an explorer, you sure like things to stay the same,' Mom said, and I guess maybe I do.

That's about it, except for one thing.

I saw X a few days ago. I hadn't seen her since the night the skinheads beat us up, but suddenly, there she was, in the park in her usual spot, waiting for me.

We met up in Allan Gardens. We sat in the greenhouse, since it was too cold to sit outside. I passed her a sandwich.

'We're moving,' I told her. 'We're leaving the city to be near my brothers.'

X looked closely at her sandwich.

'A lot has happened since we saw each other last. Everything's all packed up. We're moving in a few days.'

She didn't say anything. I complained to her about school, for old time's sake as much as anything else. She started eating.

When she was finished, I slid a folded-up piece of paper over to her. 'It's a map,' I said. 'It shows you how to find us. The secret police will never think of looking for you there.'

I stood up to go. 'Goodbye, X,' I said, holding out my hand. 'Thanks for being my friend.'

Slowly, slowly, X reached out her hand until it was holding mine.

'Goodbye,' she said. Then she picked up her blue suitcase and walked away.

Life will never be the same again. No more bothering people at weddings, no more grumpy Valerie on Saturday mornings, no more sliding peanut butter and corn syrup sandwiches across a park bench for X. But there will be other things, new things. That's how it is with change. You leave one thing behind, and there's something else to take its place.

It will be like that when I finally get to go exploring. No matter how much I like a place, I'll have to leave it behind before I can go on somewhere new.

I'm going to turn myself into a walking, talking backpack—full of pockets and secret compartments for tucking away memories of each place I visit.

And when I finally take my place in the middle of the Khyber Pass, I'll have bits and pieces inside me from people and places all over the world, and everyone who meets me will go away thinking they've met someone very interesting indeed.

Deborah Ellis was born in Northern Ontario but grew up further south, in Paris, Ontario, Canada. Like many writers, she was a creative loner as a child, at odds with formal education in her youth, and a voracious reader at all times. As an adult, Deborah has been occupied with many issues of interest to women, such as peace, education, and equality in society at home and abroad. She works at a group home for women in Toronto, Ontario, reading and writing in her spare time.

Deborah also travels whenever she can, listening to people's stories, especially the stories children tell about their lives. The children Deborah writes about really live on the page. Their vividness teaches us something about how real children and young people, in other times or in other places, might have lived or do live now, with whatever life gives them to bear.